10/22/98

For Christina,

Look out for Piddlesticks!

THE AMAZING FRECKTACLE

THE AMAZING FRECKTACLE

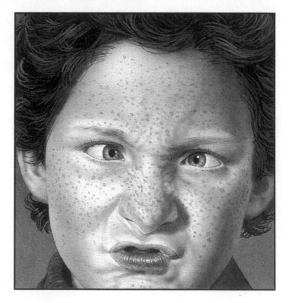

ROSS VENOKUR

Delacorte Press

Published by
Delacorte Press
Bantam Doubleday Dell Publishing Group, Inc.
1540 Broadway
New York, New York 10036

Library of Congress Cataloging-in-Publication Data
Venokur, Ross.
   The amazing frecktacle / Ross Venokur.
      p.   cm.
   Summary: A fifth-grade boy trades his 5792 freckles to a strange department store manager in exchange for a fitting revenge on everyone in school who has ever tormented him.
   ISBN 0-385-32621-1
   [1. Freckles—Fiction.   2. Magic—Fiction.   3. Teasing—Fiction.
4. Schools—Fiction.   5. Family life—Fiction.]   I. Title.
PZ7.V562Am   1998
[Fic]—dc21   98-11520
                                                                  CIP
                                                                  AC

The text of this book is set in 14.5-point Adobe Garamond.
Book design by Susan Clark
Manufactured in the United States of America
October 1998
10   9   8   7   6   5   4   3   2   1
BVG

For Mom.
Thanks for all the freckles.

PROLOGUE

A YEAR BEFORE

Nicholas Bells woke up to a screaming alarm clock. Not his alarm clock—he could have turned that off and gone back to sleep, or never bothered to turn it on in the first place and slept all day. No, it was the alarm clock in his parents' room that woke Nicholas and his younger brother, Tham, every morning—way too early to get ready for school.

While Nicholas tried to fall back asleep, his dad came in to say good-bye—just the way he did every morning. Nicholas was too tired to talk, so he just lay there with his eyes closed.

Tham, however, was wide awake in the top bunk. When Dad walked in, Tham popped up to say hello, smashed his head on the ceiling, rubbed his eyes, and started chatting away. Dad listened for a minute, gave Tham a quick kiss on the forehead, and left for work.

Had Nicholas known what that day would bring, he might have forced his tired eyes open and had one last conversation with his dad. You see, Mr. Bells left for work that day, and no one has seen him since.

INTRODUCING THE AMAZING FRECKTACLE

First thing Friday morning, Elliot Arsham's awful voice echoed through the hallways of Greenacres Elementary School.

FRIENDS, FELLOW STUDENTS, ESTEEMED FACULTY MEMBERS, STEP RIGHT UP AND FEAST YOUR EYES ON THE GREATEST WONDER OF THE UNNATURAL WORLD. DON'T BE SHY, HE WON'T BITE—AT LEAST I DON'T THINK HE WILL. LADIES AND GENTLEMEN, I PROUDLY PRESENT NICHOLAS BELLS . . . THE AMAZING FRECKTACLE!

Nicholas was no stranger to insults. He was a walking catalog of easy targets, so he'd had more than his share of teasing. Take his hair, for example. In third grade, everyone had called him *Pumpkin Boy*. No one wants to be called Pumpkin Boy, but Nicholas felt the silly name was harmless and he ignored it. But when Elliot started calling him *Jack O'Lantern*—that stung. It was too close to the truth.

You see, Nicholas's hair was a jungle of tangled orange curls—which, by the way, his mother just loved. But there was no denying that his head looked like a jack-o'-lantern sitting there right on top of his shoulders.

Well, Nicholas was a smart boy. He told his parents about his problem and then came up with a plan. He figured if he cut his hair short, no one could accuse him of looking like a gourd. And you know what? He was right.

Nicholas made it through the rest of third grade without a single insult. His classmates were stumped, even Elliot—but on the first day of fourth grade, they tried to get back in the game. Everybody called him *Funny-looking*! That was the best the kids could do. Until Elliot introduced his brand-new whopper and Nicholas became the *Wimpy Witch of the West*.

Why the Wimpy Witch? Because Nicholas had a witch eye. Which eye? His right eye. That's right, his right eye was half green and half blue with the tiniest hint of yellow.

Mom and Dad tried to tell him that the right eye meant you were a good witch and the left eye (or the wrong eye, depending on what you meant by right) meant you were a bad witch. Regardless of which eye was a witch eye, it was an easy target upon which (not witch) Elliot could sharpen his rusty wit.

But as I said, Nicholas was a smart boy, and after consulting his parents again, he devised another plan. Colored contact lenses. Instead of a multi-colored witch eye, Nicholas now had two green eyes. He figured that would leave the other kids very little to say. And once again, he was right (not like left, but more like $2 + 2 = 4$).

For a whole year, no one could find another reason to torment Nicholas. He made it through the entire fourth grade, all of the summer, and most of the fifth grade without a single nasty name. And then that fateful Friday morning rolled around when the freckle jokes began.

Nicholas should have seen it coming. After all,

he had freckles *everywhere*—freckles on his face, freckles on his shoulders, freckles on his arms, and freckles on his legs. There were three smelly freckles on the bottom of his left foot and one odd freckle in the yellow part of his witch eye—but you can't see that one anymore, because it's covered by his contact lens.

Nicholas didn't know what to do to stop the jokes this time. You can cut off your hair and wear colored contacts, but *you cannot remove a freckle.* And Nicholas had a lot more than just a freckle. He had 5,792, to be exact.

How did he know he had 5,792 freckles? Well, he sat and counted them, of course. Using a pen to color in each freckle so that he didn't count any twice or leave any out, Nicholas ended up with 5,792 tiny blue spots all over his body.

As anybody with freckles will tell you, names like Freckle Face and Polka Dot come with the territory. But who cares? That's like calling a girl with glasses Four Eyes or a boy with braces Tin Grin. As Nicholas always reminded himself, *Lame names, jokes, pokes, and teases, all blow by like harmless breezes.* He'd heard freckle jokes for so long, they didn't even count as insults in his book.

But on that Friday morning, Nicholas knew he was in over his head. *The Amazing Frecktacle.* It was catchy. Go on, try saying it. *The Amazing Frecktacle.* Feel the way it rolls off your tongue.

The new name was a big hit. Oscar Mercein, the class bully, slammed Nicholas into a locker and proudly proclaimed, "Hey you, Amazing Frecktacle!" as if he had thought of the slur himself. Poor Nicholas. Finally the morning bell rang and all the kids ran off to their classes, sparing Nicholas further abuse for the moment. But as I said, Nicholas was a smart boy, and he knew that this time he was doomed.

He couldn't go home and talk it over with his parents because Dad was gone. And Mom, well, Mom hadn't taken to Dad's sudden disappearance too well. At first she quit her job and spent days staring at the phone. She was waiting to hear from the police, who searched and searched and then searched some more. Occasionally neighbors would stop by with casseroles and other smelly things for Nicholas and Tham to poke at, but Mom hardly noticed. Her eyes were glued to the phone (not literally, of course).

Eventually the police decided that Dad must be

dead. Mom refused to believe them, though. She decided that Mr. Bells had left on purpose. She even figured out why—he hated her freckles. He'd always said he loved her freckled face, but now Mom knew that was a lie. He didn't like those ugly spots at all. So Mom decided to declare an all-out war on freckles, and things really started to change.

Mom began covering her face in makeup and dousing herself with buckets of perfume. If you ever had the misfortune of riding in an elevator with her, your throat would get so itchy that you'd actually believe you'd eaten the fur off a French poodle for supper. Your eyes would water so much that you'd wonder if the world's smallest chef was hiding in your pocket dicing onions. I'm telling you, this perfume could make a dead man gag, but it didn't seem to bother Nicholas's mom one bit.

After she "put on her face"—which meant covering her freckles—Mrs. Bells would frolic about the snootiest parts of town, buying everything she saw. Occasionally she would take a break and sit down to tea with other freckle-free women who looked, acted, sounded, and smelled just like her. These friends called Nicholas's mom Elizabeth

Dahling. Nicholas hated that name. He liked it better when people called her Lizzy.

Lizzy, or Elizabeth Dahling or Mrs. Bells or whatever you want to call her, was not about to let her sons disappear like her husband. So Nicholas and his brother had to spend all their spare time running errands with Mom. And the worst of all Mom's errands was the weekly trip to the cosmetic counter at Uppercrust and Elitist's, her favorite department store.

Maybe you've seen the commercials on TV. You know, the ones where that stodgy old bag of wind, Q. V. Uppercrust, glares at you through his ridiculous monocle, while his frumpy partner, P. W. Elitist, busily sucks on a ludicrously long cigarette holder. They chuckle, and chortle, and talk down to all of us, perpetually boasting about their "guaranteed, exclusively overpriced merchandise."

Whenever Nicholas, Tham, and Mom went to the cosmetic counter, the two ghostly pale Cosmetics Ladies were ready and waiting. Their ivory skin glowed next to the jet-black hair that draped over their faces and slid down their narrow necks. They were tall, bone-thin, elegant women, and Mom would sit and gossip with them for hours while sampling the latest products developed to cover up her "unsightly facial blemishes."

So *that's* why things were different this time. Dad was gone, Mom was not herself, and freckles were an extremely sore subject.

Mom's hatred of everything freckled weighed heavily on Nicholas as he ate his lunch, alone, hiding from everyone behind a big oak tree in the corner of the playground. He stared at his crustless sandwich and told it, "There's absolutely *nothing* amazing about being a frecktacle. Nothing amazing at all."

That's when Tham walked up. The news of Nicholas's amazing nickname had already reached way down to the second grade, and Tham knew exactly where his older brother would be hiding.

"Nicholathe," Tham asked, "ith everything okay?"

"Yeah, Tham, everything's fine."

In case you're wondering, Tham had no freckles. In fact, with his straight brown hair and brown eyes, he didn't look like Nicholas at all, which is not to say that everything was perfect in his life. Tham had a terrible lisp—you may have noticed.

Actually his name was really Sam, but no one called him that.

Tham also put the letter *n* in the wrong place. If it was raining outside, you would ask for an umbrella, right? Not Tham. He always asked for a numbrella.

Sometimes Tham tried to use words that were too big, and he'd get confused. If you saw a tall man with a neatly pressed pinstriped suit on, with a gold pocket watch dangling from his vest, you might describe him as an elegant man. But if Tham saw that same man, he'd call him a negligent man—which to Tham was the same exact thing, because he had no idea what either of those words meant.

Other times, when Tham used two big words together, he'd get all mixed up and so would his words. Once he went with Nicholas to the candy store and eagerly asked the bald, plump man behind the counter for thix cherry thixie pickth. To you, or me, or that bald, plump man behind the counter, "thix cherry thixie pickth" doesn't mean much. But somehow Nicholas knew what his brother was trying to say.

"Six cherry pixie sticks?" Nicholas asked.

"That'th what I thaid, thix cherry thixie pickth."

Nicholas always knew what Tham meant. Hiding behind that tree on Friday, Tham didn't know what to say. So he just sat there, next to his brother. But Tham couldn't stay quiet for long.

"I with Dad wath thtill here," he finally said.

"I know, Tham, I wish he was here, too."

"Who knowth? Maybe he'll come home tonight."

"Maybe."

But Nicholas knew better—Dad wasn't coming home, Mom wasn't going to change, and this problem was not going away.

2

MR. PIDDLESTICKS

Friday afternoons always dragged on forever. Nicholas stared at the clock on the wall right above his teacher's head. The closer it got to three o'clock, the longer each minute took. Finally the clock reached 2:59—the longest minute of the entire week.

2:59 and 2 seconds: Nicholas fantasized about what he could do over the weekend. He could go to the park and play roller hockey with some friends. He could see a double feature of gory horror movies. He could eat the world's largest ice-cream sundae. He could win a go-cart race and become a famous racing hero. And he could probably even make time for his homework.

2:59 and 10 seconds: Nicholas sighed as he imagined what he'd actually end up doing over the weekend. His mother would drag him and Tham around as she did her tedious errands.

"What's the difference?" Nicholas asked himself. "It's not like I have friends to play with, even if I was allowed to go to the park. Mom would never let me see one gory movie, let alone two. I can't eat ice cream because I'm lactose intolerant and milk makes me sick. I've never even *seen* a go-cart. And who am I kidding? There's no way I'm doing my homework."

2:59 and 17 seconds. A balled-up piece of paper hit Nicholas on the head. He glanced over at Elliot Arsham, who was acting far too innocent to actually *be* innocent. Nicholas picked up the crumpled paper, straightened it out, and read the message:

Make sure to watch the News tonight. There doing a local interest story on a hideous freak of nature known as YOU! Have a nice weekend, loser.

Underneath the note was a drawing of a television showing a picture of a freckled beast with horns on its hideous head, drool dangling from its crooked teeth, and an unidentifiable, nasty mess crawling out of its nose. The beast wore a sticker that read,

HELLO, MY NAME IS
THE AMAZING FRECKTACLE.

Needless to say, Nicholas was upset. However, he took some comfort in noticing that Elliot Arsham was not quite as clever as he thought. He spelled *there* wrong. If he was such an intelligent boy, Elliot would have written "*they're* doing a local-interest story," instead of "*there* doing." It wasn't much, but at least Nicholas had something to cling to.

2:59 and 28 seconds. A hand swooped down, out of nowhere, and grabbed the piece of paper that Nicholas was brooding over. The hand belonged to Mr. Gosen, his teacher.

"Well," Mr. Gosen said as he studied the note, "The Amazing Frecktacle has apparently found something more exciting than my lessons."

Nicholas's teacher was an odd man, and perhaps the strangest thing about him was that he didn't laugh, he guffawed. What's a guffaw? Have you ever been around someone who hears something so funny he turns red and chokes? That's just that person's way of laughing, but it actually looks as if he's dying. *That's* a guffaw, and when Mr. Gosen did it, smelly pieces of his lunch that had been hiding between his teeth and his gums all day would spew out of his bloated face. And that's exactly what he did as he scanned the note with his crossed eyes. He guffawed. Nicholas bowed his head in shame.

"It seems," Mr. Gosen said as a small piece of the egg-salad sandwich that he ate for lunch sailed across the room, "that one of my students is an artist. Who would like to see this wonderful portrait of the Amazing Frecktacle?"

"No!" Nicholas shouted. "Don't call me that! And don't show them! It's all his fault!" He pointed directly at Elliot, who simply said, "Is not."

2:59 and 46 seconds. Nicholas looked at the clock. "Come on," he begged. "Give it back!" But it was too late. Mr. Gosen was walking around the room, showing the drawing to the other students.

One by one, Nicholas's classmates started to laugh, until the entire class giggled, and chuckled, and chortled, and sniggered, and snickered, and snorted, and, of course, guffawed. And then, finally,

RING!!!

The bell sounded and it was the weekend.

Saturday morning, Mom dragged Nicholas and Tham out of bed to start her shopping. And guess where they went first.

"Elizabeth Dahling! It's so wonderful to see you!" Mom sat down at the makeup counter and the two Cosmetics Ladies got to work.

"Oh, dahling, do we have a product for you," the first Cosmetics Lady said.

"Covering up those disgusting spots of yours has never been easier," the second Cosmetics Lady added.

"Divine!" Mom proclaimed. "I just hate these freckles."

Tham eyed his brother in time to see Nicholas wince. A folded-up piece of paper fell out of Nicholas's pocket. Tham picked it up.

"What'th thith?" Tham asked as he unfolded the note.

"Oh, that?" Nicholas said. "Elliot did that."

"I'm thorry, Nicholathe."

"Why are you sorry? It's not like you drew it—or showed it to everyone else in class."

Tham tore up the drawing.

"Igloo it, Nicholathe. It'th thtupid."

"How can I ignore it, Tham?" Nicholas choked on his words, his eyes bulged out of their sockets, and his cheeks turned a deeper shade of red.

"I hate being the Amazing Frecktacle. I wish I could get rid of my freckles forever!"

Suddenly, as if by magic, a creaky voice interrupted Tham and Nicholas's conversation.

"Hello, boys."

Nicholas was thrown off by the sudden appearance of Uppercrust and Elitist's store manager. He barely remembered his manners.

"H-Hello, Mr. Piddlesticks."

Ah, Mr. Piddlesticks—what a character. His menacing smile made him look as if he was always imagining some new scheme. His eyes were dark, fathomless pits overshadowed by a single, bushy eyebrow—which was just as greasy and oily as the hair on his head and in his spindly mustache.

Mr. Piddlesticks always wore the same deep purple suit. He walked with a conspicuous limp, and when it was quiet, you could hear his unique steps approaching—*du-dump, du-dump, du-dump*. And what's strangest of all is that he decorated his lapel with a tiny sprig of parsley.

But you couldn't see the most noticeable thing about Mr. Piddlesticks. You smelled it. He always left the most wretched stink behind—an acrid, burning odor that lingered in your nose long after he had gone, a smell distinct from the one created by Mr. Piddlesticks's constant belching and . . . well, you know, the nastier smell that explodes from the other end. Not at all what you'd expect from the manager of such a snooty store.

Nicholas and Tham had heard a few stories about Mr. Piddlesticks. One woman claimed she saw him pull up a leg of his trousers to scratch a particularly irritating itch and she discovered that his knees were on backward.

Another woman said she interrupted a conversation Mr. Piddlesticks was having one day in the stockroom. So what? you ask. Well, he was suppos-edly having this conversation with a gruesome face that protruded from his own belly. (Incidentally, both of these women have been fired and no one has seen either of them in a long time.)

So this was the peculiar man who interrupted Nicholas and Tham on that Saturday morning.

"What are you two rascals up to?" His shrill, piercing voice hurt the boys' ears and made them squinch their faces as if they had just bitten into a lemon.

"Well, you thee, Mithter Thtiddlepickth, Nicho-lathe wath jutht thaying that he withed he could loothe hith freckleth onethe and for all."

Mr. Piddlesticks found Tham's words as confus-ing as you do. He turned to Nicholas.

"What did he just say?"

"Nothing," Nicholas mumbled. "It doesn't mat-ter."

"That's strange, because it sounded to me like he said something about you wishing you could lose your freckles once and for all. But I must have misunderstood him, because why in the world would you possibly want to give away your freck-les?"

"Because they're ugly! And if I didn't have them, maybe everyone would stop teasing me."

Mr. Piddlesticks wore his I'm-busy-concocting-a-scheme smile. "I would never make fun of someone with freckles. I simply love them."

"Really?" For a moment Nicholas was delighted. He couldn't remember the last time someone had complimented his freckles—someone besides the ever-supportive Tham, that is.

"Of course, your father didn't have freckles, and you'd probably like to be more like him." The smile on Mr. Piddlesticks's face grew wider, offering the boys a view of his yellow and brown teeth.

"Maybe," Nicholas said.

"Hey, how do you know about our dad?" Tham asked in perfect English. He always liked it when he had a chance to use sentences without *s*'s in them.

"Oh . . . he, uh, used to buy gifts for your mother here."

"Here? I doubt it. Thith ithn't the kind of plathe where our dad would have thopped."

Tham's angry glares went unnoticed by Mr. Piddlesticks, who turned his attention back to the older boy.

"I really do love your freckles," he told Nicholas.

"You do?" Nicholas asked hesitantly, fearing that he was being dragged into an all-too-familiar setup and should expect the standard putdown to follow.

Magically, all Mr. Piddlesticks did was nod. He really meant it. "In fact," he stated, "I want them."

"Yeah? Well, I wish I could give them to you, but unfortunately, I can't."

"Oh, but you can, my boy. You can."

"Trust me, Mr. Piddlesticks, if there was a way to get rid of freckles, I would know about it. You're just making fun of me like everybody else does."

"If you're really so sick of your freckles, don't you at least owe it to yourself to hear me out?"

The smile on Mr. Piddlesticks's face grew even larger, and Tham swore he could see between the rotten teeth all the way back to the little pink ball dangling between Mr. Piddlesticks's tonsils. This conversation was getting a little too strange for him. But Nicholas seemed intrigued.

"Um, Nicholathe," Tham said, tugging on the back of his brother's shirt, "I think Mom ith ready to leave."

"Nicholas"—Mr. Piddlesticks dangled his offer in front of the boy's face like a huge hunk of cheese in front of a tiny, starving mouse—"I can make your freckles disappear . . . forever."

"Yeah, right."

"It's true. Besides, what's the harm in trying?"

"I'll think about it," Nicholas said.

Mom's nasal voice broke through. "Kids! Come on, we're leaving."

"Think all you want, Nicholas, but my offer expires tonight at exactly one minute past midnight."

Mom started to walk away and Tham tugged harder on Nicholas's shirt. "Let'th go," he demanded.

"If you'd like to take me up on my offer," Mr. Piddlesticks instructed, "all you have to do is open this satchel and do what you're told." He handed Nicholas a small brown pouch.

"Nicholas! Tham!" Mom hollered across the crowded store. "Now!"

Nicholas looked over at Mom. When he turned back a second later to say good-bye, Mr. Piddlesticks was gone. All that remained was the awful stench, which seared Nicholas's twitching nostrils, and the small brown bag Nicholas clutched in his hand.

THE SATCHEL

Mom dragged her two boys all over town as she ran her stupid errands. Nicholas kept himself busy contemplating the incredible possibility of freckle removal—though he didn't mention it once because he knew the whole business bothered his brother.

Tham spent the entire time telling awful old jokes, like this one:

MOTHER GOOTHE, OLD HOTHER MUBBARD, AND MAMA MIA ALL WALKED INTO A BAR, WHICH ITH THRANGE BECAUTHE YOU WOULD THINK THAT after Mother Goothe walked into it, the other two would have ducked.

Nicholas didn't get it, but Tham laughed at how clever he was—until Nicholas put him in a head-lock and gave him noogies. When Mom couldn't take the commotion anymore, she yelled, "Cut that out!"

The day seemed endless for all of them.

That night as he got ready for bed, Nicholas couldn't concentrate on anything. He was too busy thinking about things like freckles and their absence. He didn't even notice that he was drooling toothpaste all over himself. Tham's giggles finally broke through his freckle-induced trance.

"What's so funny?"

"Look at yourthelf, doofuth."

Nicholas wiped the slimy gunk off his face.

"All right, boys," Mom screamed from her room down the hall, "bedtime."

Nicholas and Tham crawled into bed and went to sleep. Well, that's not entirely true. Tham went to sleep. Nicholas stared at the ceiling. It was ten o'clock, and he only had two hours and one minute to make up his mind.

The decision seemed easy enough. Nicholas hated his freckles and couldn't get rid of them. Mr. Piddlesticks loved freckles and said he could take them. So that was that. Nicholas would take Mr. Piddlesticks up on his offer.

There was, of course, another side. Should Nicholas trust this mysterious man, who was no more than a stranger? And what about those stories about Mr. Piddlesticks? Besides, everyone knew there was absolutely no way to get rid of freckles. So, once again, that was that. He would forget the whole business and go to sleep.

But an hour later, Nicholas was still staring at the ceiling, thinking about life as the Amazing Frecktacle. His mind flashed forward to future milestones of his life. He imagined the far-off day when he would get a driver's license—only the license wasn't registered to Nicholas Bells. It was registered to the Amazing Frecktacle.

He imagined hearing the dean of students calling the Amazing Frecktacle to the graduation platform to accept his college diploma. Nicholas would have to trudge up and collect the certificate as his classmates and their families pointed and sneered.

He imagined the part of his wedding when the justice of the peace would say, "Do you, the Amazing Frecktacle, take Cara to be your lawfully wedded wife?" That is assuming, of course, that he married someone named Cara. But do people named Cara marry people named the Amazing Frecktacle? Probably not. He would end up marrying someone named Tanya Tin-Grin, or something like that.

Finally Nicholas imagined being dead, sleeping in his coffin, forever aware that sitting six unreachable feet above him was a headstone chiseled with the inscription HERE LIES THE AMAZING FRECKTACLE. A SPECKLED MONSTER. REST IN PEACE.

Worst of all, more horrible than anything else, and painful to think of, Nicholas imagined Elliot Arsham. And finally, *that* was that.

He looked at the clock. It was ten minutes to midnight. There was still time.

Nicholas quietly slunk out of bed, stumbled around, and found the satchel.

"It can't hurt to try," he told himself. He opened

the pouch and fished out a small glass tube filled with an iridescent yellow liquid.

"What is this?" he asked himself.

He put it down on his desk and looked in the satchel again. There was something else—a folded-up piece of paper, thick and yellowed with age. Beautiful script, written in a raw red ink, covered the outside:

Piddlesticks and candlewicks
showered to toe with dark black tricks
will make himself a spectacle
to service the Amazing Frecktacle.

Nicholas unfolded the paper and discovered a message:

Nicholas, my boy, do as I tell you: Crack an egg on a mirror and pour the tube of rhinoceros stomach acid into the yolk. Clear your throat, collect a big wad of phlegm, and when the yolk fizzles, spit on it!

"That's disgusting," Nicholas thought. Was Mr. Piddlesticks for real? Did he really want Nicholas to spit into an egg? Only one way to find out. Nicholas ran to the kitchen and grabbed an egg out of the refrigerator. Then he snuck into his mom's bathroom and borrowed one of her many vanity mirrors.

He was all set. But when he returned to his room, the vial was not where he'd left it.

"Hey, Nicholathe, what ith thith thtuff?" Tham had woken up and opened the vial.

"Tham, put that down, right now." Nicholas's voice trembled. Tham obeyed his brother.

"You shouldn't touch that, Tham. It's not for you."

"Why not?"

"You're too young."

"Tho?"

"So, I don't want you to get hurt."

"Hurt? Nicholathe, what'th going on? Thith hath nothing to do with Mithter Thtiddlepickth, doeth it?"

Before Nicholas could answer, the bells on the local church started to ring. It was midnight. Nicholas had only one minute left. The time for thinking was over.

He cracked the egg and watched as it plopped

29

down onto the small mirror. Nicholas grabbed the vial of acid from his confused brother and dumped it into the bulbous yellow yolk. The mixture fizzled, but the faint crackling noise was instantly drowned out by Nicholas's phlegm-gathering. And then *Spittew!* Nicholas hocked a loogie all over Mom's mirror.

Tham and Nicholas stood there. Tham was completely baffled by his brother's weird behavior. But Nicholas didn't do anything else. He was waiting for something to happen. Nothing did.

"I was right. Piddlesticks was just teasing me. I'm such a sucker."

Suddenly something happened, as if to prove Nicholas wrong. A hot draft rolled through the room, and a rat scurried out from a pile of dirty laundry. Nicholas and Tham jumped up onto their beds.

A cold draft blew in, and two snakes slithered out from underneath the same laundry pile.

Then a puff of smoke.

Tham coughed.

Nicholas's eyes watered.

An excruciatingly long second passed.

The smoke cleared.

The rat and the snakes were gone.

Mr. Piddlesticks and two women stood in their places. The women's long black hair looked familiar to the boys, but who in the world did they know who wore deep purple and black gowns with parsley corsages pinned to their chests and black knee-high boots?

Mr. Piddlesticks was the first to speak. "Nicholas, my boy, I can't tell you how thrilled I am that you decided to take me up on my offer."

Nicholas and Tham were speechless. They didn't know what to do. What if their mom walked in right now? She would kill them. They weren't even allowed to have friends in their room, so they could forget about strangers.

"Hasn't your mother taught you that it's impolite to stare?" Mr. Piddlesticks asked. "Besides, I believe we all know each other here, don't we?"

One of the ladies spoke. "Hello, Nicholas."

"Hello, Tham," the other added.

And then, together, they asked, "How is your mother? She's such a dahling."

"Huh!" Nicholas gasped. He recognized the

women—the Cosmetics Ladies. He had never seen them look so happy. And for a moment he feared that their brilliant white teeth would blind him.

"So, Nicholas," Mr. Piddlesticks interjected, "are you ready to get rid of your freckles forever?"

Mr. Piddlesticks's smile grew so wide that Tham thought it might actually split his head in half. Neither of the boys made a sound.

"I'll take that as a yes."

THE MAKEUP
COUNTER

Mr. Piddlesticks snapped his fingers, and Nicholas found himself standing outside his apartment building staring at two pure black stallions with purple saddles. The Cosmetics Ladies were nowhere to be seen, but Nicholas didn't notice—he had bigger things on his mind.

"Well, Nicholas, I'm about to give you everything you've ever wanted. Saddle up."

Though Nicholas's brain was busy sending out frantic fear signals to every part of his body to demand an immediate flight from danger, his heart was pounding out a stronger message—"This is it!" Nicholas was thrilled. "Wow," he thought. "My wish is going to come true." He hopped up onto one of the stallions, but before his mount took its first step, Tham came bursting outside, totally out of breath from running down all the stairs.

"Oh, no," Nicholas said, "where do you think you're going?"

"With you and Thtiddlepickth," Tham panted.

"No, you're not."

"Amtoo."

"Arenot."

"Amtoo!"

"No way," Nicholas declared. "You're staying home."

"If I thtay," Tham threatened, "I'm telling Mom."

Mr. Piddlesticks was not amused by this brotherly banter. "Nicholas, we must do this while the moon is still empty," he insisted, pointing up at the sky. Nicholas looked up. The moon really was empty—exactly the opposite of a full moon.

Nicholas turned to Tham, who clearly had no intention of letting his brother ride off alone with this twisted department-store weirdo. "Fine." Nicholas caved. "You can come, but don't leave my side."

Mr. Piddlesticks's menacing smile returned to his crooked face. "Excellent."

And with that, Mr. Piddlesticks jumped on his horse. He sat backward in his saddle and kicked the horse with the heel of his pointy shoe, causing it to rear up on its hind legs and gallop down the street. Nicholas and Tham's beast chased after its companion.

It was the middle of the night and there was scarcely a car on the road. Occasionally a taxi would drive by and the driver would rub his eyes to make sure that he wasn't seeing things and that there were really two boys and a peculiar man galloping down Madison Avenue on jet-black stallions.

The horses ran at incredible speeds, and Nicholas was exhilarated. If the other kids could see him now, they would not insult him; they'd praise him. They'd call him brave and adventurous. Elliot Arsham could never muster the courage to hurtle full speed down dark streets on a mighty stallion.

The strange caravan whizzed past a hunched-over doorman asleep on a chair outside his building. A street cleaner appeared and disappeared again. Streetlights buzzed. Nicholas thought how nice it would be if the magical ride never ended, if he could just gallop into tomorrow and tomorrow and tomorrow.

But the ride finally came to an end—in front of

Uppercrust and Elitist's department store. The boys dismounted and the stallions morphed into the two Cosmetics Ladies.

The odd group entered the store.

Mr. Piddlesticks stopped at the makeup counter.

"What are we doing here?" Nicholas demanded. "You said you would get rid of my freckles forever, not cover them up with makeup."

"Patience, my young friend. Everything is not always what it seems."

"All I want is to never hear the name Amazing Frecktacle again as long as I live."

"Say no more." Mr. Piddlesticks laughed. Not laughed, actually it was a bit more than a snicker but not quite a cackle, perhaps a snackle. Then he snapped his fingers, and the floor behind the makeup counter disappeared, revealing a long, winding, stone staircase. The stones were covered in a putrid slime that smelled like moldy cheese. The group descended the steps, traveling beneath the makeup counter, beneath the store, beneath the city, and into Mr. Piddlesticks's lair.

They entered a dungeon filled with books, bottles, filth, and occasional moans of despair that seemed to emanate from nowhere. Mr. Piddlesticks moved across the stone floor, which was covered in the same moldy, old-cheese-scented slime as the stairs, toward one of the many shelves that lined three walls. Three ominous statues stood against the fourth wall. They were statues not of people but of creatures, or maybe they were monsters, or maybe they were just things—horrible, horrible things.

Each statue was more confused than the next. One had an alligator's head but a bull's body with human arms—six human arms. The second looked like a winged dragon, with a sickeningly large bloodshot eyeball for a head. The third was the worst of all, the head of a beaten-up tiger, the ears of a baby elephant, the tentacles of a giant squid, the body of a horse, and a tail unlike any I have ever seen.

"All right, Nicholas," Mr. Piddlesticks began, "here's the deal. In exchange for every single one of your freckles . . . by the way, how many freckles do you have?"

"Five thousand, seven hundred and ninety-two."

"Exactly? No more, no less?"

"Exactly 5,792. I counted myself."

"Good. So in exchange for the 5,792 freckles

that you counted yourself, I will exact revenge on every single snot-nosed kid who ever tormented you—starting with the leader of those horrible brats, Elliot Arsham. After all, you know what I always say: *Lame names, jokes, pokes, and teases, demand revenge through bad diseases.* So what do you say, Nicholas, do we have a deal?"

Nicholas, a bit overwhelmed by the evening's events and more than a bit frightened by the dank, musty dungeon, was trying hard not to cower before Mr. Piddlesticks. He heard his own heart pounding as he gathered up every bit of courage in his body and stared Piddlesticks in the eye.

"Yeah, we have a deal."

The conviction in his voice took everyone by surprise, especially Tham, who was far less brave in the presence of such foreboding company. Tham's knees shook, his teeth chattered, and his hands sweated—most likely from gripping the tails of his brother's shirt so tightly.

Mr. Piddlesticks produced a scroll from inside his purple coat. He unrolled it for Nicholas, who instantly recognized the raw red script printed on the page. It was a contract.

Standard Freckle Contract

LET IT BE KNOWN
THAT IN EXCHANGE FOR SECURING THE
FIVE THOUSAND SEVEN HUNDRED AND NINETY-
TWO FRECKLES THAT NICHOLAS BELLS (PARTY A)
HAS COUNTED ON HIS OWN BODY,
MR. PIDDLESTICKS (PARTY B)
WILL EXACT A FITTING REVENGE UPON EACH
AND EVERY ONE OF THE SNOT-NOSED KIDS
WHO HAS EVER TORMENTED PARTY A;
AND PARTY B WILL BEGIN THE REVENGE
WITH ELLIOT ARSHAM,
A PARTICULARLY SNOTTY SNOT-NOSED KID.
AGREED TO THIS DAY BY

X_____   X_____
NICHOLAS BELLS   MR. PIDDLESTICKS
  (Party A)   (Party B)

Have a Pleasant Day

One of the Cosmetics Ladies handed Mr. Piddlesticks an unusual pen. "This lovely instrument is made from the petrified body of a six-hundred-year-old earthworm," he told the boys, who now expected no less from this bizarre man. Mr. Piddlesticks signed the contract and handed the pen to Party A.

Nicholas took a deep breath.

Tham gripped his brother's shirt tighter.

Mr. Piddlesticks snackled.

Nicholas grabbed the gruesome pen and signed the contract. (Secretly Nicholas was relieved that he was only signing a contract and not solving a word problem. He was happy that he didn't have to figure out whether Party A or Party B would arrive at the train station first.)

Mr. Piddlesticks's smile disappeared. He rolled up the contract and tucked it into his jacket, under the purple lapel and parsley sprig. He grabbed a huge leather-bound manual from a shelf and dropped it onto the tabletop, where it landed with a thud. A cloud of dust billowed up into Tham's nose, causing him to explode in a chorus of powerful sneezes. Mr. Piddlesticks ignored the ruckus and leafed through the manual. "Ah, yes. Here it is," he said as he thumbed through the pages, "Chapter Ten: Freckles."

One of the Cosmetics Ladies used a piece of ordinary chalk to draw two circles on the ground—one inside the other. The second Cosmetics Lady scattered parsley inside the border created by the two circles.

"Ith that parthley?" Tham innocently inquired.

The Cosmetics Lady nodded.

"Why are you thprinkling it on the ground like that?"

"Because, you feebleminded little fool, parsley is the most powerful plant in the world." (I feel compelled to point out that I am only relating the events and dialogue as they occurred and that just because one of the Cosmetics Ladies called Tham a feebleminded little fool doesn't mean that he is one. In fact, I happen to believe that Tham is quite intelligent and that he was being rather brave given the situation and his age.)

"Motht powerful plant in the world?" Tham challenged. "Come on."

The Cosmetics Lady went about her business.

41

However, studies have shown that intelligent minds yearn for the truth and, as I just told you, Tham had an extremely intelligent mind. He demanded an answer.

"Why'th it such a nunusually powerful plant?"

"Because, you impertinent little brat, it must travel to Hell and back before it germinates."

That didn't make any sense. And it certainly was not what Tham or Nicholas wanted to hear. Things were crazy enough underneath the department store without someone bringing up Hell.

"Um, you know what, Mr. Piddlesticks?" Nicholas suddenly reconsidered. "Maybe this isn't the best idea. Why don't we just, uh, well, call this whole thing off?"

"No dice, Nicky," Mr. Piddlesticks snapped. He clearly had no intention of bending. "You signed the contract. Now get in the center of those circles and shut up."

For the first time all night, Nicholas was completely, thoroughly, 100 percent terrified. What had he gotten himself into? And worse, what had he gotten Tham into?

"I'm sorry," Nicholas explained, "but I think that I want to go home."

Mr. Piddlesticks glared down at Nicholas. "I don't care what you want."

One of the Cosmetics Ladies grabbed Tham. Mr. Piddlesticks's dreadful smile sealed the deal— and he was blocking the stairs as well. Nicholas had no choice. He stepped into the center of the circles. Tham did the only thing he could: He stood there with a record-sized string of drool dangling from his wide-open mouth.

Mr. Piddlesticks pulled down a number of vile vials from his shelves and dropped them into a filthy pot. The glass vials shattered in a crescendo of crashes, and a thick, pulsing substance bubbled over the top of the pot.

Mr. Piddlesticks snackled so loudly that it sounded like a roar. He dropped one final ingredient into his concoction and then stirred the mess as he spoke:

"Piddlesticks, oh Piddlesticks,
severed earth worms, headless ticks,
throw in thirteen slimy slugs,
and then add seven unknown bugs.
Add a cockroach to the mix,
blend it all with three swift kicks.

Sprinkle over with nasty germs
from a poodle with a perm.
Seal it off with lizard licks
and let the spirits start their tricks.

"Moldy slime, now hear my plea,
this boy's freckles belong to me!
Pluck them off from his nose,
his arms, his legs, his back, his toes,
don't forget to check his knees,
dot your i*'s and cross your* t*'s.*
You now know what to do—
five thousand seven hundred ninety-two!
It's simply the way things must be,
certifiably dastardly."

"Noooo!"

Who said that? It wasn't Nicholas, who stood in a daze, or Tham, who was scared stiff, or Mr. Piddlesticks, who was busy snackling, or the Cosmetics Ladies, who beamed with delight, which leaves a question—who else was in that dungeon? It sounded as if the voice came from the alligator-headed statue, but that was simply impossible. And at that moment, it really didn't matter, because something much more disturbing was happening. The murky, moldy-cheese-scented slime that covered the floor began to move.

The slime hummed and vibrated and pulsed and wiggled until it grew so agitated that it broke into pieces, rose up, and took shape right before the boys' eyes. Nicholas found himself surrounded by legions of slimy, ripe-cheese-scented gobbledygooks—and I promise you that these were most definitely not friendly slimy, ripe-cheese-scented gobbledygooks who were just coming by to say hello and make a friend.

No, what followed was the single scariest experience of Nicholas's life. The slime converged on him and plucked off every single one of his 5,792 freckles, one by one. Tham couldn't even see Nicholas. He was lost in the tides of the freckle-picking, old-cheese-smelling slimy ocean.

For those of you have never experienced a legion of slimy gobbledygooks picking off your freckles one by one, let me assure you that you feel no pain. But each time a freckle is ripped off, there is a faint popping sound. Imagine that you are Nicholas, and all you see are hundreds of blobs lunging and grabbing freckles off your body, and all you can hear is *pop, pop, pop, pop, pop, pop, pop, pop, pop* (I'll let you put in the other 5,783 *pops* yourself); and all you can keep telling yourself is that you asked for this—no, you prayed for this. It's quite traumatic, wouldn't you say?

Luckily for Nicholas, just as quickly as all of this grim gobbledygook nonsense began, it ended. The slimy creatures filed past Mr. Piddlesticks, dropping the freckles in a small sack he wore around his neck before they disappeared into the floor, the walls, and the steps.

Nicholas Bells stood dumbfounded inside the chalk circles. He looked at his arms. He pulled up the legs of his pajama pants and looked at his legs. He looked across the room at a mirror and saw his face. Mr. Piddlesticks had done it!

Nicholas Bells's freckles were gone.

The Amazing Frecktacle was no more.

5
WARTS

"**T**ham, look at me! Look at me! No freckles! Ha ha!" Nicholas grabbed his brother and waltzed around the room.

What was Tham thinking? Was he as happy as his brother? Not exactly.

Picture someone you know who has freckles. It doesn't matter who; anyone with freckles will do. It could be that girl with the funny tooth who sits behind you in math class, or the grizzly bus driver who takes you to and from school every day, or even that gawky teenager who works at the ice-cream store and always sneezes in the Double Peppermint Whizzle Road. Just pick a person and imagine his or her freckled face in your head. Got it? Good.

Now comes the tricky part. Picture that same freckled person, only this time picture her without the freckles. Everything is exactly the same, only no freckles. Get it? Your friend looks pretty strange, huh? When you remove freckles from a freckled person, it looks as if something is missing.

People do obvious things to change their appearance all the time. Some people put on phony fingernails and gaudy wigs. Other people have cosmetic surgeons suck out all their fat or cut their noses in half. You yourself change your appearance every time you cut your toenails or get a haircut. But afterward, no one would say, "I'm experiencing the strangest sensation, I feel like you should have more hair." Most likely, someone would say something like, "Haircut?"

You'd say, "Yep."

He'd say, "Looks good."

And you'd say, "Thanks."

However, if a freckled friend shows up one day without freckles, I guarantee you'd be completely baffled. You wouldn't know what had changed.

You might sense something was missing—nothing as obvious as an arm or a leg, but something else— something that you can't quite put your finger on. A freckled person with no freckles looks remarkably incomplete, strange even.

"Tham, isn't this the single most marvelously wonderific thing that has ever happened to us?" Nicholas asked as he danced around the dungeon. "Isn't it? Isn't it?"

Tham was in an awful predicament. How could Nicholas think he looked good? He looked more like . . . well, like a freak.

"It ith, Nicholathe."

So Tham didn't really believe that, but he was not about to ruin Nicholas's moment. The Cosmetics Ladies, on the other hand, were.

The Cosmetics Ladies giggled. Actually it was more than a giggle; it was painfully higher, more of a piercing sound. Perhaps we'll call it a piggle. Through the screeching racket of their irritating piggling, one of the ladies urged Mr. Piddlesticks, "Go ahead, tell him."

"Yeah," the other one added, "let him know what a fool he is."

Mr. Piddlesticks shot the women a grave look that said, "Shut up." But it was too late. Nicholas had heard them.

"Tell who what?" he asked.

"Oh, never mind those two giddy birds. They're always speaking out of place." Mr. Piddlesticks redirected his attention to his new freckles.

Nicholas wasn't prepared to back down yet. "Who's a fool, Mr. Piddlesticks? Me?"

"Nicky, Nicky, Nicky, I got rid of your freckles just like I said I would. So why don't you run along home and enjoy your new life?"

"No." Nicholas put his foot down. "I deserve to know what's going on here."

"Says who?" Mr. Piddlesticks's voice bubbled over with impatience. "You're in my world now, Nicholas Bells, and you deserve what I say you deserve. Take my advice, you and your brother should do yourselves a favor and skedaddle." But Nicholas was not ready to leave. He wouldn't budge.

Mr. Piddlesticks snackled.

"Adamant little snot, aren't you? I admire that. Here's a free tip: A fool should never ask what makes him a fool. The answer is always upsetting.

But if you must know, I'll tell you. Your freckles—excuse me, *my* freckles—are powerful. More powerful than anything you could ever imagine."

"Powerful?" Nicholas had his doubts. "You're trying to tell me I have magic freckles?"

"No, I *am* telling you that you *had* magic freckles and now they belong to me."

"But there's no such thing as a magic freckle."

"Oh, really?" Mr. Piddlesticks's voice was getting higher and higher. "Why do you think I offered to remove your freckles? To be nice?" The Cosmetics Ladies piggled. "And why do you think I made you sign that contract? Because I wanted to help you get revenge on a group of insignificant children?"

Actually Nicholas hadn't thought about it. He had been so focused on getting rid of his freckles that he'd never bothered to ask why Mr. Piddlesticks was willing to take them. Everyone knew that Nicholas would have done anything to get rid of his freckles. He'd have given them away for free. Heck, he would have paid someone to take them.

"Why *did* you make me sign that contract?" Nicholas asked nervously.

"Because, and not that I expect a stupid boy like

you to understand anything that I say, magical forces have rules and laws that govern them just like everything else in this universe. Nothing is as random as it appears."

"So?" Nicholas wondered.

"So," Mr. Piddlesticks went on, "you cannot simply take someone else's power. You have to trade for it. So I traded revenge on your tiny tormentors for your glorious freckles. Without a trade, your freckles would do me no good, because they would still belong to you. The contract makes our deal official—and unbreakable. And thanks to our little agreement, these freckles are officially mine forever."

"And they have magic powers that only you can use?"

Mr. Piddlesticks's jagged smile spread across his face. "Exactly."

Nicholas still didn't believe what he was hearing. "Prove it."

Tham jumped nervously at his brother's words. There was no way that Nicholas had just asked Mr. Piddlesticks to prove it, was there?

"Very well," Mr. Piddlesticks answered, "but

only because I'm feeling a little giddy. Remember—you asked for it."

Tham took this as his cue to dive under a table and hide.

Nicholas stood still, waiting for nothing to happen, but a little worried that something might.

Mr. Piddlesticks narrowed his eyes and spoke:

"Magic freckles, newly acquired,
seek the boy from whom you've retired,
sprout a third arm on his head,
hairier each day until he's dead
so that he'll never have reason to doubt
the awesome forces that flitter about."

Mr. Piddlesticks looked at his sack of freckles, ready for fireworks. But as Nicholas had suspected, nothing happened. And when I say nothing happened, I do not mean it the same way that I meant it every other time I said, "Nothing happened"—you know, only to be followed up a sentence or two later by telling you that something fantastic actually did happen. This time, all kidding aside, nothing happened.

"Hey, Tham." Nicholas spoke with new confidence. "I think it's safe to come out now." Tham, still a little nervous, hesitantly stuck his head out from underneath the table.

"I don't understand!" Mr. Piddlesticks was furious. He did not like being made to look stupid in front of anyone, especially small children whom he was attempting to impress.

"Perhaps I can explain, Mr. Piddlesticks," Nicholas suggested. "My freckles . . . they were ugly, not magic."

"No! It can't be." For the first time all night, Nicholas got to laugh at Mr. Piddlesticks, who suddenly had very little to snackle about. In a fit of rage, he refocused and tried another spell:

> *"Magic freckles whose powers are strong,*
> *track the boy to whom you belonged.*
> *Make his nose a chewed-up carrot,*
> *his personality, a mute parrot's.*
> *Alter him on my behalf,*
> *to teach this snot when not to laugh."*

54

Tham held his breath and waited for Nicholas's nose to change. But once again, nothing happened.

Nicholas was thoroughly unimpressed. "Come on, Tham, we better head home and give Mr. Piddlesticks some time to figure out how to use his *magic* freckles." Tham sensed that the danger was over, and crawled out from underneath the table. Just to be safe, he grabbed his brother's freckleless hand.

Mr. Piddlesticks lifted his eyes from the sack around his neck. He glared at the two boys, standing side by side in front of him. The smile, that awful, scheming smile, returned to his face.

"What?" Nicholas demanded. Mr. Piddlesticks did not answer.

"All right," Nicholas bargained, "you had your fun. We were scared, really. Now, if you could just tell us how to get out of here . . ."

"What's the rush?" Mr. Piddlesticks asked. "You two should stick around, and I'll tell you why. I just had a positively, devilishly brilliant idea. The freckles will not harm you, Nicholas, because you nurtured them, you gave them life, a body to grow and thrive on."

"Okay, whatever you say. Can we leave now?"

"Not yet; not until you witness their incredible power."

"But I thought you just said that the freckles can't harm me because I nurtured them, or grew them, or whatever you just said."

"You're right. That's what I said. They won't hurt you. But," Mr. Piddlesticks continued, "that doesn't mean they won't go after little ol' Tham, here." When Mr. Piddlesticks started to snackle, Tham wished he had not resurfaced from underneath the table. Tham looked at Nicholas for some reassurance, but even he looked queasy.

Mr. Piddlesticks's voice rang through the room:

"Magic freckles, three's a charm,
the older boy is free from harm,
which only leaves our little friend Tham
as the target of our last KA-BAM!
Sorry, kid, but I will not abort
until you're cursed with hideous warts."

This time, I regret to inform you, something did happen. The sack around Mr. Piddlesticks's neck came to life. The strings untied themselves, and

56

Nicholas's freckles stormed out. They flew in two perfect parallel columns and headed straight for their trembling target, Tham. Paralyzed with fear, he didn't even attempt to dodge his attackers. And to be honest, it would not have made a difference if he had.

The freckles covered Tham's body, settling for less than a second before returning to the sack. Nicholas looked Tham over, up and down, all around. As far as he could tell, nothing had changed.

"Don't worry, Tham, he was just trying to scare us again, but if we don't . . ."

Nicholas didn't finish his sentence. He couldn't finish his sentence. He was preoccupied with the sudden activity on Tham's face. You see, right above Tham's left eye, the skin split apart and made room for a raw growth to emerge. Dozens more bumps formed—on Tham's nose, his cheeks, his ears, his arms, his hands, his legs, his shoulders, and his back. A vile wart formed on every single spot that a freckle had touched. Within seconds, Tham had 5,792 warts.

There are few things in the world grosser than a wart, and these were not your average, everyday, small, hard lumps. These were worse. They were thick and wide, and each one glistened as if it was coated in cooking oil. Pus fizzled and popped from them like lava from active volcanoes. The warts vibrated. They seemed alive, as if they were trying to escape from Tham's body. But I promise you, these vulgar, swelling viruses were not going anywhere.

Mr. Piddlesticks snackled.

The Cosmetics Ladies piggled.

All three of them vanished.

A hot draft rolled through the room, filling Nicholas and Tham's nostrils with Mr. Piddlesticks's rank stench.

A cold draft blew in, and Nicholas and Tham blinked and found themselves back at home, in their own room.

6

MOMMY AND MUMMY

Sunday in the Bells's apartment was a nightmare. It was not at all how Nicholas had imagined his first freckle-free day would be. Mom was in bed with a nasty flu, and every so often she would let loose a deep moan, signaling Nicholas to come running. She wanted OJ, or water, or another garbage pail to vomit into.

Mom was so sick that she could barely lift her head without the room spinning. Her shades were drawn, her lights were off, and her eyelids were far too heavy to open, all of which allowed Nicholas to slip in and out of her room without questions like "What happened to all your freckles?" and "Where is your brother?" Which raises an interesting question. Where was Tham all day?

In the bathroom, retching at the sight of his own face, of course. And that's where Nicholas was when he wasn't holding Mom's head over the trash can.

"Nicholathe," Tham pleaded, "I look like a nalligator. Do thomething. I can't go to thchool like thith."

Nicholas knew he was in way over his head. But he played it cool for Tham's sake. "Let's concentrate on your face, okay? If worst comes to worst, you can wear a long-sleeved shirt and pants to cover up the rest of the warts."

"What about my handth?"

"You'll wear gloves, I guess."

"To thchool?"

"Look, do you have a better idea?"

"Don't get mad at me." Tham's voice rose. "Thith ith all your fault."

"What's that supposed to mean?"

"It'th thuppothed to mean that you called Mithter Thtiddlepickth and you thigned the protract!"

"The contract?"

60

"Whatever, Nicholathe. You think everyone wath mean to you when you had freckleth? Jutht wait until they thee me."

"Calm down, Tham. It's not that bad."

Tham wasn't buying Nicholas's cool-and-collected act. "Lithten, if I thtill look like thith tomorrow, I promithe that I will hate you forever." Red with rage and wet with tears, Tham stormed out of the bathroom, leaving Nicholas behind.

Nicholas caught a glimpse of his freckleless face in the mirror. He raised his hand to his cheek and touched it. Something wasn't quite right, but he didn't know what. "Better go talk to Tham," he thought. As he walked back into his room, something caught his eye. He looked over at his bookshelf and saw his stuffed cheetah. It had been his favorite toy. His father gave it to him on his seventh birthday.

"For *my* spotted cheetah." That was what Dad had said.

"You loved my freckles," Nicholas now thought. "I would never have been stupid enough to give them away if you stuck around, Dad." A lonely tear rolled down his cheek.

"Oh no," Nicholas cried, and ran back to the

bathroom. Standing in front of the mirror with his freckleless hand resting on his equally freckleless cheek, Nicholas realized what was so wrong about his face. No freckles. He wasn't Dad's spotted cheetah anymore.

An awful, gut-wrenching moan came from his mom's room. Nicholas hurried down the hall to see what she wanted.

After he'd helped Mom, Nicholas changed into his pajamas and got into bed. Tham was sobbing into his pillow.

"Tham?"

No response.

"Tham? Come on, talk to me."

Silence. Nicholas had betrayed his little brother, his best friend, and his only ally in the world.

"I won't let them make fun of you, Tham. I promise."

Monday morning Nicholas woke up early. Mom was still sick, and he moved about the house freely, preparing for Tham's day at school. By the time Tham woke up, Nicholas was ready.

"Look, Tham, I know you hate me, and I don't

blame you, but I'm still your older brother and I am not going to let anyone see you like this."

Tham was trying to act mad because he was supposed to hate his brother from now on. "What'th your plan?"

"Well," Nicholas said, "I'm going to cover up your warts."

"What about tomorrow? or the next day? or the day after that?" Tham had clearly been hoping for a better plan.

"I'll just keep covering them up until they go away."

"Do magical warth go away, Nicholathe?"

That was an interesting question. Nicholas didn't know, but that didn't stop him from answering.

"Of course they do." Tham actually believed Nicholas and felt a little better. After all, Nicholas was still his big brother, even if Tham was committed to hating him for the rest of time.

"What are you going to uthe to cover them with?"

"This." Nicholas unrolled several long pieces of gauze. "Get dressed. Put on these pants and this shirt of mine—the sleeves will be extra long on you. Then we'll wrap your head and your hands in the gauze."

"That won't work. The minute clath thtarts, Mith Martin will make me take it off."

"Not after she reads this." Nicholas pulled a note out of his pocket.

Miss Martin:

My son Tham had an unfortunate run-in with an open canister of toxic waste this weekend. I, for one, was absolutely convinced that his face was going to melt off, but Dr. Nelson assured me that Tham's hideously gruesome face and hands will eventually heal. In the meantime, he must wear dreadful medicated iron-fiber bandages at all times or, as Dr. Nelson said, "he will risk contaminating his fellow students and everyone else within a fifty-foot radius of the poor, wretched creature." Thank you for your understanding of this sensitive issue.

Sincerely,
Elizabeth Dahling

The handwriting matched his mom's perfectly—as well it should, considering Nicholas had spent all morning writing and rewriting it.

"You think it'll actually work, Nicholathe?"

"Why not? Now, go on, get dressed, so I can wrap you up."

Nicholas and Tham approached the main gates of Greenacres Elementary. Every inch of Tham's body was covered, save two tiny eye holes and a slit for his mouth.

"I feel thtupid."

"What are you talking about, Tham? You look great."

"Yeah," Tham said as he studied one of his wrapped hands through his eyeholes, "I look great for a three-thouthand-year-old dead Egypthian. Everyone'th thtill going to teathe me, you know."

"No they won't, Tham, because you'll tell them that if they tease you, you'll unwrap your bandages and contaminate all of them, and then their faces will melt off, too. If they ask Miss Martin whether you're lying, she'll tell them all about the note from Mom. Trust me, no one will bother you."

"That's right, Tham, your older brother got you

into this mess, and he'll get you out of it. Isn't that right, Nicky?"

"Mr. Piddlesticks?" Nicholas asked in disbelief.

True enough. Mr. Piddlesticks was lurking about the main gate, waiting for Nicholas and Tham. He still wore his purple suit and his wilted parsley corsage, and as his demented smile spread across his gnarled face, a burst of gas shot from his bottom.

"You were expecting the Queen of England, perhaps?" A half-snackle at his half-witted joke was all Mr. Piddlesticks could afford. Other students began to arrive and file past Nicholas, his mummified brother, and the oddly out-of-place Mr. Piddlesticks.

"Why are you here?" Nicholas asked.

"A deal's a deal. I would never dream of welshing on our contract."

Across the schoolyard, a small cluster of students was forming around Elliot Arsham. He directed their attention to Tham, the innocent victim of strange circumstances.

"Look, it's okay," Nicholas all but begged, "I'll let you out of the deal. Just go away."

"Sorry, kid, but it's not that simple."

Elliot's growing mob began to move across the yard toward Nicholas and Tham.

"You've caused enough trouble for us," Nicholas implored. "Now, please, leave."

"You obviously don't understand what I'm trying to tell you, you dumb kid," Mr. Piddlesticks asserted. "If I don't live up to my end of the deal, I'll have to return your freckles to you, and we all know that only a dimwitted fool would willingly give away his magic. Look, it's time to pay back all those little snots who've tormented you. Why don't you try to enjoy it?"

Mr. Piddlesticks disappeared into the crowd of students, which abruptly stopped behind its leader, Elliot. He stood face-to-face with Nicholas. For a moment, Nicholas didn't notice Elliot. His eyes were fixated on a rat that was scurrying into school.

Elliot shoved Nicholas. That caught his attention.

"Leave me alone, Elliot." Nicholas's voice was exhausted. "I'm not in the mood."

Elliot didn't care. "You didn't actually think you could come to school looking like this and not have to answer to me." Nicholas's heart sank in his chest.

Here it comes, the barrage of mummy jokes. Poor Tham took a step back and tried to hide behind his brother, hoping he could act as a shield and deflect the insults.

The crowd grew quiet. Name-calling was Elliot's department. Some kids claimed that he was put on this Earth for one reason and one reason only: to make up names. It was his specialty, and out of respect, everyone waited for him to throw the first insult of the morning. He cleared his throat, cracked his neck, stretched out his arms, and let it fly.

"Look, everybody, the Amazing Frecktacle finally did something about those ugly liver spots he tries to pass off as freckles. He covered them up with girly makeup. I guess now we should call him *Frecklette*."

The crowd of students burst into laughter.

Oscar Mercein, the simple-minded putz, yelled, "Yeah, or maybe we should call him *Girly*."

The painfully dull Anabelle Edwards screamed, "or *Makeup Boy*." Other students quickly joined in with equally inane contributions. And all the while, Nicholas and Tham stood there, baffled. Was it possible that the students of Greenacres Elementary had grown so dependent on their habit of insulting Nicholas that they did not even notice the three-foot-tall mummy standing beside him?

The bell rang. The students gave up, for the moment, and went to class.

Tham was, of course, thrilled that no one had commented on his bizarre state. But he was also sad for his big brother. No matter what he did, Nicholas could never catch a break. Tham reached up and patted Nicholas on the shoulder before wandering off to his class. He wanted to say something, but really, what was there to say?

Nicholas lingered behind, contemplating what had just happened. He stared up at the imposing school. This wasn't how it was supposed to be.

The second bell rang. A dark cloud that reeked of Mr. Piddlesticks loomed above as Nicholas trudged off to class.

7

ROLL CALL

Nicholas slunk in through the door at the back of his classroom and was surprised to find chaos. Kids sat on their desks talking. Elliot Arsham belittled two innocent computer geeks in the corner. One particularly homely kid, Tom Thomas, was lying on the floor sleeping. And there was no sign of the teacher.

With the efficiency of an android's built-in tracking system, Elliot noticed Nicholas and instantly shifted his attention to the recently renamed Frecklette, user of girly makeup. He was about to tear into Nicholas when Principal Aaron entered. The short, stout, confused-looking man cleared his throat to let his presence be known and to signal the students to find their seats.

"Children," the principal said in his matter-of-fact voice, "I have bad news. Mr. Gosen has come down with a nasty case of chicken bocks, not to be confused with chicken pox. This is, of course, extremely strange since, as far as I can tell, there is no such disease as chicken bocks.

"However, when a man calls you and can't get a single word out without bocking like a chicken, my policy has always been, don't ask questions. Especially considering that Mrs. Gosen then got on the phone and explained that her husband has a beak and wings, and that he's growing feathers at a remarkable rate. As I've been known to say from time to time, the last thing I need is a huge chicken running around my school.

"Anyway, there's no need to be concerned. As far as I can tell, chicken bocks is probably no more contagious than, say, the black death was in the Middle Ages. Heck, in one year that disease only got to fifteen percent of England's population. But if any of you happen to grow a beak, I would suggest letting the nurse take a look at it.

"In the meantime, you will all be happy to know that we have arranged for a brilliant substitute while Mr. Gosen is out. That said, everyone please give your new teacher the same respect that you afforded Mr. Gosen."

The substitute entered. Nicholas blinked hard. No wonder Mr. Gosen had suddenly come down with a disease no one had ever heard of. Principal Aaron cleared his throat again.

"Class, this is your new teacher, Mr. Piddlesticks." The principal made a swift exit, leaving the class under the watchful eyes of their sinister substitute. Mr. Piddlesticks picked up the attendance book, gave Nicholas a quick wink, and addressed his students. "When I call your name, stand up, come to the front of the room, face the class, and answer one question. It's an exercise to help me get to know each of you." He glanced at the attendance book. "Let's start with . . . hmmm, let's see . . . Elliot Arsham. You're first."

Elliot stood before his class.

"So, Elliot, tell us all what you did last night."

"Well, I hung out, I ate dinner, I watched TV, I brushed my teeth, and I went to bed."

"Fascinating. Really." Mr. Piddlesticks's menacing smile danced on his face. "Elliot, why don't you tell us what you did after that."

"After I went to bed? I slept."

"And after that?"

Elliot was caught off guard by Mr. Piddlesticks's probing questions. He began to blush and fidget. Nicholas actually felt bad for Elliot, so unaware of the true nature of his new teacher. But what could Nicholas do now? He had to wait and see what Mr. Piddlesticks was up to.

"Come on," Mr. Piddlesticks continued, "you can tell us. We're all friends here." Elliot's face turned a deeper shade of red.

"Um, I—I . . . don't know what you mean."

"Come now," Mr. Piddlesticks insisted, "you had a dream, didn't you?" Elliot remained silent. "And in that dream, what did you become?"

Mr. Piddlesticks had really struck a chord because Elliot Arsham, tough guy, tormentor, name-caller extraordinaire, began to cry, right there in front of the whole class.

"It's okay, Elliot. If you don't want to tell us, why don't you just show us?" As Mr. Piddlesticks spoke, a freckle flew out of his sack, heading for Elliot. The freckle landed delicately on Elliot's cheek, carefully sidestepped a teary puddle, then spun around and jumped back into its sack. Elliot's face suddenly changed. It was covered in makeup—girly makeup. His lips were bright red, his cheeks a pretty pink, and his eyes—his eyes were painted with the loveliest shade of blue, glittery shadow.

More than anything, Elliot wanted to escape the cruel laughter of his classmates, but he couldn't lift his feet. He looked down and saw that his high-tops were gone, replaced by yellow high heels. Then he saw that his jeans were gone—he was wearing tights. And horror of horrors—he was wearing a dress. But the most surprising thing of all—especially for Elliot—was when he opened his mouth to say "Shut up," but instead found himself saying, "Just call me Elliette," in a shrill voice. The class exploded into more laughter. Revenge was under way.

Suddenly and all at once, the other kids turned to Nicholas in the back of the room. Wasn't this the very moment that the Amazing Frecktacle had been waiting for his whole life? A chance to lead an attack on "Elliette" Arsham?

Nicholas thought it over. He knew this was

payback time. But he couldn't even squeeze out one tiny insult to complement this humiliating moment. Archenemy or not, this was all wrong.

"Little wimp, can't even enjoy his own party," Mr. Piddlesticks sputtered under his breath. "All right, class. Settle down. Elliette, feel free to stay right there as long as you like. Your tears become you. Now, let's see, who shall I call on next? Hmmm. Is Oscar Mercein here?"

"Here." Oscar stood up and made his way to the front of the class, stepping around pretty Elliette and his fountainous eyes.

"So, Oscar, why don't you go to the board and do some simple long division for us? I want you to put one into one hundred."

Simpleminded Oscar grabbed a piece of chalk and wrote $1 \div 100$ on the board. He stood there and stared for a minute. Then he scratched his head. Then he took a step back to get a different view of the problem. Then he glanced over his shoulder to see his class, which was silently giggling.

"Oscar, you helpless creature," Mr. Piddlesticks sneered, "there isn't much going on upstairs, is there?"

"Upstairs? Well, how should I know, I haven't been upstairs today."

"That's not what he meant, you nitwit," Tom Thomas shouted. It was too much for the others to handle. They broke out into violent laughter. A freckle tapped Oscar on his big dumb head. A second, more powerful explosion of hilarity occurred when the top of Oscar's head became completely transparent, revealing that he actually had a pea-sized brain.

"What?" Oscar demanded. "What's so funny?"

"Your head!" the awkwardly tall Frankie Stein shouted. "Look at your head, birdbrain!" Oscar studied his reflection in the window. He reached up and touched his invisible cranium. It felt fine. The most intelligent kid in the world would not have known what to make of this situation, so you can only imagine how confused this nitwit was. He did the only thing he knew how to do: He imitated the others, joining them as they laughed at him.

"Enough," Mr. Piddlesticks announced. Oscar's puny brain managed to send a signal to the rest of his body, and he sat down. Anabelle Edwards was called on next, and, being too dull to suspect a thing, she bounced to the front of the room.

Before Annabelle returned to her seat, a freckle would cause an enormous zit to mysteriously form on the tip of her nose, right in the middle of her lecture on the importance of being cute. The zit exploded all over the front row of desks and then started to form again, only to explode and re-form and explode and re-form and so on.

Nicholas grew more agitated as one by one, each of his classmates approached the front of the room, sidestepped Elliette, the prettiest boy alive, and innocently received Piddlesticks's punishment. Why should Nicholas care what happened to them? Why? He shouldn't. But he did.

Stinky Stan Martin, the boy who always smelled like a wet dog, could thank a freckle for forcing him to run around on all fours and drool out of his newly formed snout.

Two freckles tackled the problem of vertically splitting in half Rodney and Samantha Wooderhausen, the fraternal twins, and putting them back together the wrong way. They were now identical twins, each one half boy, half girl—100 percent mixed up.

All it took was the lightest tap of a freckle to turn Frankie Stein, the tallest bully in class, into a two-foot-tall punching bag. It was a dream come true for the short kids in the class, who took turns kicking him around.

Gossipy Gabby Boca was in the corner talking to herself—a freckle had truly given her the gift of gab. She now had fifty pairs of lips all over her body that wouldn't stop talking about who was dating whom, and who was wearing what, and whose parents were getting divorced, and who'd been caught kissing in the closet.

Another freckle turned the already unattractive Tom Thomas into something of a monster. Hair sprouted out of his ears, his nostrils, and the five moles that graced his oddly shaped face.

Nosy Bill Kim was nosier than ever now that a freckle had turned his nose into an absurdly long elephant trunk.

But at least he still had his nose. The freckle that attacked Susan Boyle, the girl who could never stop sniffling, was not as kind. Her runny nose hopped off her face, sprouted legs and feet, slipped into a pair of running sneakers, and took off.

Mr. Piddlesticks just kept on going. And what's worse is that the kids kept on teasing each other. Nicholas couldn't bear it anymore. Couldn't they see that this was wrong? A dog-faced boy shouldn't make himself feel better at the expense of a girl with fifty pairs of gossipy lips. A kid who can't even catch her own nose certainly has no right to insult someone else's honker. But the insults flew.

Looking around, Nicholas was faced with one awful fact: This was all his fault. He had brought this evil man into the school. And it was now his responsibility to stop him before he really went too far. But how?

"What am I going to do?" The question bounced around inside Nicholas's skull. He needed some peace, some quiet, and some time to think. He ducked out the back door. Mr. Piddlesticks was having far too much fun to notice.

8

CONSEQUENCES

While Nicholas wandered aimlessly through the labyrinthlike hallways of his school, he reviewed his troublesome predicament.

He had been re-renamed Frecklette—which, though it may not be worse than Amazing Freck-tacle, was certainly no better. Tham, his brother, was covered in warts and wrapped in gauze. Mr. Gosen, his teacher, was suffering from some non-existent disease. His classmates were turning into a huge side-show attraction. And it was all his fault.

All he had wanted was to get rid of his freckles, forever. He didn't know the price would be so high. He stopped in front of a display case and studied the reflection of his freckle-free face.

"And the worst part," he told himself, "is that I look ridiculous without my freckles." He finally understood that boys and girls with freckles have freckles for a reason—however elusive that reason may be. Elliot Arsham was actually right; Nicholas did look as if he was wearing makeup, sort of.

Nicholas ambled over to Tham's class and spied through the back window. The teacher was lecturing to a roomful of kids who were doing what students always do. Some paid attention, and some fidgeted in their seats. Some chewed gum, others blew bubbles. Some slept with their heads in their arms, others with their noses in the air and their mouths wide open, collecting dust. And not one of them sat anywhere near Tham, the banished Mummy Boy.

Well—would you sit next to him? Honestly? Would you really sit next to a boy who'd had a run-in with an open canister of radioactive material? No, you wouldn't. I don't care what you think you'd do, I'm telling you that there's no way in the world you would ever sit next to a contagious, toxic classmate.

It killed Nicholas to see his brother sitting alone, isolated like a hermit whose lifestyle had been thrust upon him. The warts, the fabricated toxic encounter, the gauze, the loneliness—none of it was Tham's fault. It was Nicholas who had asked for change, not Tham.

Nicholas took a deep breath. Couldn't anyone help him? Mr. Gosen was a giant chicken, and even if he could stop bocking long enough to get a word out, Nicholas would never seek help from anyone who called him the Amazing Frecktacle. Mom—well, Mom had been a lost cause since Dad disappeared.

"Dad," Nicholas thought. He would have done anything to speak with his father. Dad was big, and strong, and smart, and there was no problem he couldn't solve. What would Dad tell Nicholas to do in this situation?

Nothing, because Dad would never have let Nicholas get himself into this situation. Dad loved freckles. He used to joke that the only reason he'd married Mom was her freckles.

Completely lost, Nicholas looked into the class again and watched two boys pass a note back and forth. One of them drew a picture on a piece of paper and handed it to the other, who added to the drawing before passing it back. The boys giggled under their breath and held the drawing up so that others could appreciate their masterpiece. It was a sketch of Tham, the Mummy Boy, with his bandages removed to reveal a grotesque, melted face.

Without taking a second to think about what he was doing, Nicholas stormed into the classroom. "Excuse me, Ms. Martin." Nicholas had no idea what he was going to say until the words were actually coming out of his mouth. "Um, Principal Aaron asked me to tell you that he, um, wants to speak with you and the rest of the teachers for an emergency faculty meeting in the . . . gym."

"When? Now?"

"Yeah, it sounded important, something about cutting back teachers' salaries, or something like that. I don't know."

"Oh, dear Lord." Ms. Martin grabbed her handbag and ran out of the class, heading straight across the small campus toward the gym.

Nicholas turned on the two boys who were passing the note. He grabbed it from them and tore it up.

"What'd you do that for?" one boy hollered.

"Yeah," the other one added, "what's your problem, huh? This doesn't concern you."

"Doesn't concern me? Doesn't concern me? Idiots like you have been teasing me my entire life. Are you so perfect? You with your huge nose . . ."

The one with the big nose bowed his head to hide the offending appendage.

"And you with your fat fingers . . ."

The one with the chubby fingers sat on his hands.

"Maybe everyone should call you guys Dr. Nose-a-lot and his clumsy assistant, Sausage-hands?"

The two boys suddenly had nothing to say. Their classmates just laughed. Nicholas turned on the pack of mindless hyenas. "Don't laugh—you with the big ears, or you with that birthmark on your cheek, or you with the frizzy hair—"

Dr. Nose-a-lot stood up and interrupted. "Ignore him. He's just mad that he comes from a family of freaks. I mean, look at him, he's an Amazing Frecktacle who thinks he can actually fool us by wearing girly makeup . . ."

The vein on Nicholas's forehead bulged.

". . . and who has a diseased mummy who can barely speak the English language for a brother . . ."

Dr. Nose-a-lot was caught up in the moment and did not notice Nicholas's jaws clenching together in fury as he approached the edge of restraint.

". . . and whose dad is dead—or maybe he just couldn't handle being married to that snobby wench, Elizabeth Dahling."

Nicholas cannonballed over the edge of restraint. "Listen, you eagle-beaked, AstroTurf-haired, sweaty-pitted, cross-eyed onion-breath of a twit"—another ounce of pressure and the dams holding back Dr. Nose-a-lot's tears would have surely burst, letting loose a tidal wave—"if you say one more word about my family, I'll—"

"What? You'll what?" Dr. Nose-a-lot whimpered.

"I'll . . ." and Nicholas had to think about this because he really had no idea what he would do. The truth is that he probably would have done nothing, but that hardly makes for an effective threat. "I'll—I'll . . ." Nicholas never had the opportunity to finish that thought because Dr. Nose-a-lot, in a last-ditch effort to hold on to his pride, picked up a book and hurled it at Nicholas's head.

The book connected with a *whack* and sent

Nicholas tumbling to the ground. Dr. Nose-a-lot's lame pride did a shoddy job of covering up his fears: that Nicholas was older and bigger, that his parents would be furious when they found out that he threw a book at another boy's head, and that Miss Martin might walk in at any second.

Nicholas rubbed his head and stared at the book. Tham, who until now had been attempting to stay out of the fight, helped his brother up.

"Doeth it hurt, Nicholathe?"

"What?" Nicholas was distracted. He couldn't take his eyes off the book that was lying on the floor. It was a text book, *Dr. D. J. Chung's Complete English Grammar Manual.* "Does what hurt?"

"Your head," Tham said, "obviouthly."

"Huh? My head? My head's fine." Nicholas's mind was not in that classroom anymore, and he wasn't thinking about insults or big-noses or bruised heads. Visions of the department store danced in his head.

"The book!" Nicholas realized. If Mr. Piddlesticks was teaching class, the black magic manual must be sitting underneath the makeup counter, unguarded. "I can fix everything," Nicholas told himself. "Go, go, go, go!"

"Are you thure you're okay?" Tham asked. "It doethn't theem like it. You're acting thort of thtrange."

There was no time to answer. Before going to Uppercrust and Elitist's, Nicholas had to make sure that Mr. Piddlesticks was completely occupied. Nicholas ran out of the classroom and sprinted through the hallways, back to his own class.

He walked into the classroom and marveled at the collection of human oddities that he'd called his classmates. He had entered another world, one of twisted carnival freaks. Mr. Piddlesticks's voice rang through the room.

"NICHOLAS BELLS, STEP RIGHT UP AND WITNESS THE UNIMAGINABLE. STANDING BEHIND ME, IS IT A BOY OR IS IT A GIRL? IT'S NEITHER AND BOTH! IT'S ELLIETTE ARSHAM, THE PRETTIEST BOY ALIVE!

"TO YOUR RIGHT, BEHOLD A TRULY RARE SIGHT. TWO MUTANTS PONDERING THEIR LOTS. ONE HAS TOO MUCH OF A GOOD THING, THE OTHER TOO LITTLE! WHY, IT'S THE HIDEOUSLY HAIRY TOM THOMAS AND OSCAR MERCEIN, THE DIZZYINGLY DUMB BRAINLESS WONDER.

"TO YOUR LEFT, DON'T GET TOO CLOSE OR IT

MIGHT TRY TO EAT YOU. YOU MAY REMEMBER HIM
AS THAT FAT KID WHO USED TO SIT NEXT TO YOU,
BUT NOW HE'S JUST A GIANT SET OF CHOPPERS AND
A STOMACH. I PRESENT TO YOU PAUL BELCHER,
THE WALKING, TALKING DIGESTIVE TRACT."

There wasn't a single "normal" kid left in the room. Mr. Piddlesticks had cursed them all. Legs were where ears should be, lips and elbows were all mixed up, necks were far too long, extra heads were stuck in all sorts of spots, kidneys and livers were on the outside, and everything was covered in freckles. The irony of that final touch did cause Nicholas a brief chuckle—nothing compared to Mr. Piddlesticks's unique snackle, which now filled the room.

Nicholas stood face-to-face with the purple-clad ringmaster. "Oh, Nicky, Nicky, Nicky, I'm afraid you've missed all the fun." Mr. Piddlesticks flashed his dirty yellow teeth. Nicholas met that nasty smile with one of his own, which shocked Mr. Piddlesticks.

"What's this," Mr. Piddlesticks inquired, "a smile? I was expecting some more whining or perhaps some effort to convince me that"—and now

Mr. Piddlesticks imitated Nicholas—" 'it's just not fair, Mr. Piddlesticks, this isn't what I bargained for.' "

"Of course it's fair." Nicholas pretended to be excited. "They asked for it. Insult the Amazing Frecktacle and it will come back to haunt you ten-fold." Nicholas cackled with glee.

"Nicholas, I misjudged you. You're a perfectly rotten child after all, and guess what."

"What?" Nicholas indulged Mr. Piddlesticks.

"I love that about you."

"I love that about me too." They shared a snackle.

"Well, my boy, my work is done here. It was a pleasure doing—"

"You're not done, Piddlesticks, you've only just begun. Sure, you've finished with this one class, but through those doors is an entire school filled with kids and teachers who have, at one time or another, insulted me. And we both know what happens if you don't punish them all. I get my freckles back."

"Very clever, Nicky. Of course I'll live up to my end of the bargain. Don't worry. But I'm telling you, one man should not be allowed to have this much fun." And with that, Mr. Piddlesticks marched off to spread his own particular brand of joyful terror through the school.

It wasn't Nicholas's intention to subject the rest of the school to Piddlesticks's sick man's whims, but he needed to buy himself some time. If all went according to plan, Nicholas would recover his freckles and undo all Mr. Piddlesticks's mischief. Gambling with other people's lives is never a good idea, but it was Nicholas's only chance to fix everything else that had gone wrong.

THE SALE

According to the colossal clock suspended above the impressive department-store doors, it was 1:37 when Nicholas finally made it to Uppercrust and Elitist's. In exactly one hour and twenty-three minutes, school would let out and Mr. Piddlesticks would return to the store.

The plan was simple: go to the makeup counter, make the floor disappear, sneak into Mr. Piddlesticks's lair, locate the manual, look up freckle retrieval, and follow the instructions. There was only one real problem, as I'm sure you've noticed: making the floor disappear. "I'll figure it out when I get to the makeup counter," Nicholas told himself. He headed inside, where an unexpected obstacle awaited him.

"Mom!" What was she doing there? She had no business shopping; she should have been in bed with her eyelids glued together.

"Dahling," one of the Cosmetics Ladies told her, "sorry to drag you out of bed in such a state, but we knew you'd be dying to see this."

"Don't be ridiculous." Mom sniffled. "No illness in the universe could keep me away from a guaranteed, foolproof freckle-covering system."

Nicholas needed time alone at that makeup counter, but Mom and the Cosmetics Ladies were capable of gossiping for hours. He watched as their mouths moved in unison. How was it possible that any of them heard a single word when all three talked at once, no one listening, not even to themselves?

"Blah, blah, blah," one said.

"Yadda, yadda, yadda," another added.

"Iggidy, iggidy, iggidy," the third agreed. This could go on forever.

Nicholas needed to create a diversion great enough to rip these three women away from the thrilling world of gossip, chitchat, and freckle remedies. What could possibly be that exciting? Nicholas brainstormed but came up with nothing more than a light drizzle of lousy ideas.

Time was running out. If Nicholas didn't find a way around his mom, his classmates—and, more importantly, his brother—were doomed to a life of circus performances and guest appearances on daytime talk shows. There had to be a way.

He looked to his left and saw some customers shopping. He looked to their left and saw more customers. He looked to their left and saw even more customers. An idea was trying to form in his mind. Everywhere Nicholas looked, more customers. So? So! And then it hit. The great idea.

So it may not have been the most brilliant plan, but there was a chance that it might work. At the back of the store, there was a black door labeled SECURITY. Nicholas stormed into the small room.

Two fat security guards swiveled around in their crickety chairs. One had a half-eaten eclair sticking out of his jowl-like mouth; the other wore a pastry all over his dingy uniform. Eclair Mouth inhaled the remainder of his snack and licked the chocolate frosting off his cheeks with the longest tongue Nicholas had ever seen. Finally he spoke.

"Yeah?"

"I want to report a crime!" Nicholas announced. Dingy Pants perked up.

"A what?" Eclair Mouth asked.

"A crime," Nicholas repeated. "You know, two bad guys with guns in this store right now."

The guards jumped out of their seats. Well, they would have jumped, but they were too fat. So they pushed down on the armrests of their chairs, creating the most awful creaking noise you could imagine. Then they shimmied around to dislodge their oversized rears from the padded seats. Then they pushed down on the bruised and aching arms of the chairs once more. And right before the chairs were about to give up, the two guards popped out of their seats. Eclair Mouth took this opportunity to get at a scratch on his bum that had been bothering him for hours.

He huffed, "What do these bad guys look like?"

"They're an old couple," Nicholas responded, "probably sixty or so. I saw them outside. He put a gun into his pants and she put one in her purse. Then they whispered to each other and walked into the store. I bet they're gonna rob the place."

Nicholas was being clever, you see, because on

weekday afternoons scads of old people with nothing better to do wander around stores like Uppercrust and Elitist's for hours. Really, it's true. Eclair Mouth and Dingy Pants would have their hands full if they had to search every old couple in the place.

"Thanks for the tip, kid," Dingy Pants said.

The guards put on their hats, which were easily two sizes too small for their gargantuan heads, and waddled out of the room in pursuit of the bad guys. A moment later, Eclair Mouth waddled back in, grabbed a couple more pastries, shoved them in his pocket, and left again. Finally Nicholas was alone in the security room.

Sitting on the desk in front of him was the microphone for the store's P.A. system. Nicholas grabbed it, cleared his throat, flipped the switch, and in his most grown-up voice, began to speak:

"ATTENTION, UPPERCRUST AND ELITIST'S SHOPPERS AND EMPLOYEES. THIS IS YOUR FEARLESS LEADER, Q. V. UPPERCRUST, WITH A SPECIAL ANNOUNCEMENT OF AN UPPERCRUST AND ELITIST'S FIRST. THAT'S RIGHT, FOR THE FIRST AND LAST TIME EVER, WE WILL BE HOLDING A SALE ON ALL

EXCLUSIVELY OVERPRICED MERCHANDISE LOCATED ON THE TOP THREE FLOORS OF THIS STORE. THIS UNADVERTISED SALE BEGINS RIGHT NOW AND ENDS WHEN I SAY SO—SO YOU'D BETTER HURRY! THANK YOU FOR YOUR ATTENTION."

Satisfied with his first public address ever, Nicholas headed back through the ghost town that had once been the first floor. His plan had worked. Years and years of overhearing customers complain that Uppercrust and Elitist's never had sales paid off. Frantic shoppers and employees alike who were suffering from the highly contagious disease known as sale fever had already run upstairs to get the best buys. Of course Mom and the Cosmetics Ladies took the bait too.

It was 1:59, and Nicholas stared at the floor behind the makeup counter. "Now what?" he asked himself. How had Mr. Piddlesticks made the floor disappear? Oh yes, he'd snapped his fingers. So Nicholas did the same. *Snap.* Guess what. It didn't work.

Next Nicholas rifled through all the drawers and shelves behind the counter, hoping to find a key, or a keyhole, or maybe just a clue. Unfortunately, all he found was makeup. Lots of makeup. He slid down to the floor and hugged his knees. The clock was ticking.

"I wish I still had amazing freckles right now," Nicholas said out loud. "Then I'd be able to command the stairs to appear. All I'd have to do is wave my hand around and say something like:

"Freckles, make the floor disappear,
show me the stairs I know are here.
Answer me in my desperate hour
and lend me some of your awesome power."

It was quite fortunate that Nicholas was sitting where he was when he commanded his missing freckles, because when he finished speaking, the beauty products scattered all over the floor next to him and fell down the slimy spiraling staircase. The floor behind the makeup counter had actually disappeared.

"I can't believe that worked!" Nicholas exclaimed. Some shoppers and employees were returning to the main floor. "Okay, then, moving right along," he said as he headed down the stairs.

Just before he disappeared into the floor, he saw his mother staring right at him.

"Nicholas?" she asked herself. She rubbed her eyes and looked again. Her son was gone. "Darn flu, now it's got me seeing things."

As soon as his head was beneath ground level, the floor closed above him and Nicholas stopped dead in his tracks. He took a deep breath and almost gagged on the stale-cheese odor. He gathered his courage, commanded his knees to stop knocking into each other, straightened his shoulders, stuck out his chest—just like Superman—and descended into Mr. Piddlesticks's lair.

10

THE WITCH EYE

The filth, the shadows, the slime, the odor, the moans, the shelves filled with strange objects, the three hideous statues, and the manual—none of it had changed. This was not a place where you would ever want to end up alone. But Nicholas was on a mission: This was his chance to make right all he had messed up. He advanced toward the book, praying that it held the key to the mystery of Mr. Piddlesticks's black magic.

Nicholas slowly stretched his hand out toward the manual, afraid that a magic alarm system would lock him down and signal Mr. Piddlesticks. Having no other choice, though, Nicholas squeezed his eyes shut and let his hand fall onto the cover of the book. He peeked—nothing happened. Really, I mean it. Mr. Piddlesticks had not booby-trapped the manual.

With adrenaline flowing, Nicholas opened the book and flipped to Chapter X: Freckles. The chapter was long. It could take him hours to finish it, but he had less than forty minutes.

"Oh well," he said, and then he dove right in, searching for the great secret of magic freckles. If you are a boy or girl with freckles, or you know any boys or girls with freckles, you may want to pay close attention to this next part.

Not all freckles are magic. In fact, a magic freckle is the single rarest of all magical items in the known universe. How then, you must be asking, did Nicholas have 5,792 of them? He didn't, that's how.

A single magic freckle, called a Gewgaw, on any part of any person's body acts as a mystical generator that invests every other freckle on that body with power. So Nicholas had only one truly magic freckle, which fed the rest their energy. But which one was it? They all looked the same. Which of his 5,792 abandoned freckles was the Gewgaw?

The manual contained an interesting fact about

the enchanted freckle. It stated that magic freckles can never, ever, under any circumstances, be used against the person who possesses the Gewgaw. But if Nicholas had given Mr. Piddlesticks all 5,792 of his freckles, how was he able to avoid the evil spell?

"Is it possible," Nicholas wondered, "that Mr. Piddlesticks missed one of my freckles?" No, of course not. Gobbledygooks that rise from slime on the floor must be very thorough servants.

"Why won't the freckles harm me? What am I not understanding here?"

He read on, but there was little more about the Gewgaw. Nothing that Nicholas read made any sense. He was disturbed by the inconsistency between the manual's magical laws and the reality of his situation.

"Maybe," Nicholas told himself, "I had more than 5,792 freckles and I just didn't know about it."

Once again he ruled that out. He had marked each one of them with that blue pen to make sure he didn't count any twice or leave any out, and when he was done he had had 5,792 blue spots all over his . . .

And, that's when he realized where the overlooked piece of this puzzle lay.

"Of course! You can't stick a blue pen in your eye!"

Nicholas had never counted the freckle in his witch eye—the one hidden by his green contact lens. Things were beginning to make sense now. Mr. Piddlesticks's contract was for the 5,792 freckles that "Nicholas Bells has counted on his own body." Nicholas had never counted the Gewgaw, so Mr. Piddlesticks never got his hands on it. No wonder his makeshift magic spell had made the floor behind the makeup counter disappear. I mean, come on, Nicholas Bells possessed the single most powerful magic in the world.

He ran over to the mirror, bowed his head, and removed the contact lens from his eye. He raised his head and smiled at the sight of his half-blue, half-green eye—the one with the tiniest hint of yellow and that strange-looking freckle.

"Which eye is the witch eye makes all the difference." Nicholas laughed to himself. "Contract or not, there has to be a way to reclaim my freckles."

He threw himself back into the book and

skimmed the remaining pages of Chapter X, not stopping until he found exactly what he was looking for. And there it was, the answer to all of his problems. Since Nicholas still had the Gewgaw, there was a way for him to regain control over the other freckles. If he could draw exactly 5,792 dots on his body and then say the magic spell, the spots would turn into the real freckles with all their power.

It was thirteen minutes until three. Nicholas grabbed the only pen he could find, the one made from the body of that six-hundred-year-old petrified earthworm, the same one he had signed the contract with.

"I hope this works."

And with that, he plopped down onto the ground and got to work.

1.
2.
3. . . .
5,640.
5,641.
5,642.
5,643. . . .

Before he could draw freckle number 5,644, Nicholas's ears abruptly perked up and stood at attention. Those moans—there was something different about them all of a sudden. Well, not *all* of them, just one of them.

"What *is* that?" he asked himself.

It wasn't really a moan and it wasn't quite a word, but someone was saying something, and Nicholas, who thought himself all alone, could not help feeling a little nervous.

It spoke. "Ihgginath."

"What?" Nicholas whispered. "I can't understand." Who, or what, was that indecipherable moan coming from? Nicholas turned to the three statues along the wall and studied them as if he expected them to come to life.

The voice spoke again. It said . . . a name.

"Nicholas."

How could that be? Nicholas stuck his fingers in his ears and tried to clean them out.

"Nicholas."

No. He was hearing things, right? Like when you're home alone and every sound becomes something it's not. Nicholas put down the petrified earthworm, stood up, and stared into the eyes of those three grotesque statues.

"Hey!" he shouted. "Where—what are you?"

"Nicholas," the voice answered.

There was no denying it that time. The voice had clearly called out his name, and it was coming from the alligator-headed statue. Nicholas approached the stone creature, balled up his hand into a trembling fist, and pounded on the beast.

"Hello?" Nicholas asked.

"Nicholas."

Now the voice sounded as if it was coming from the monster with the oversized eyeball for a head. Determined to discover what was calling him, or to just shut it up so that he could get back to drawing the last 149 freckles, Nicholas squeezed behind the alligator-headed statue. There was almost no room between the sculpture and the wall, so Nicholas was wedged in there pretty tightly.

He took a deep breath and then, with all his strength, used his legs and pushed off the wall straight into the back of the statue, making it teeter forward ever so slightly. Capitalizing on this small progress, Nicholas pushed again.

One more deep breath and one final heave and the statue finally crashed to the ground. Nicholas expected to hear it scream, "Noooo," as it tumbled to its death. Or perhaps it would suddenly come alive and stick out those six arms to break its fall. But what actually happened was so unbelievable that Nicholas could never have predicted it.

The statue shattered on the ground, sending chunks of stone and marble all over the room and causing a cloud of dust to billow up and blind Nicholas. Unprepared, he inhaled and gulped down a huge mouthful of the dust. He started coughing like a maniac.

But when he caught his breath, the coughing did not stop. Someone else was in the room—lost somewhere in that dusty cloud. When the dust settled, Nicholas could not believe his own eyes. Someone was clawing out of the shattered remains of the statue. It was a woman.

She stretched out her arm, and Nicholas helped her to her feet. Weak, most likely from her time frozen in that stone vault, she fell back to the ground as her knees buckled. She stared up at Nicholas and started to cry.

"I'm sorry. I was only trying to help you. I'm sorry," Nicholas pleaded.

She just cried.

"Why were you calling my name?" Nicholas asked.

"I wasn't calling your name. Who are you?"

Now Nicholas was completely confused. "What were you doing inside that thing?"

"All I said was that his knees were on backward," she sobbed. "I didn't mean anything by it."

And then again, "Nicholas."

Nicholas quickly wedged himself behind the second statue—the winged one with the oversized, bloodshot eyeball for a head. He sprang off the wall and knocked that freaky sculpture over onto its side. The statue smashed into the floor, sending more rubble and dust everywhere.

With no time to spare, Nicholas jumped into the thick of the mess to see what this beast was hiding. A hand grabbed his leg. Nicholas reached down and latched on to a second woman who was struggling to emerge from the remains of the mutant eyeball.

"Who are you?" Nicholas demanded.

She just sobbed.

"Who are you?" Nicholas yelled.

As she choked on the dust and her own tears, the frightened woman's words stumbled out of her mouth. "All I said was that he has a face on his belly. And he does!"

"Nicholas," the voice screamed out.

"Out of the way, lady," Nicholas snapped as he pulled her over to the other woman. He wedged himself behind the third and final statue—the confused creature with the head of a beaten-up tiger and the body and limbs from nature's smorgasbord. He stirred up his remaining energy and sent that mess crashing down to the floor.

Marble fragments shot across the room. The dust compounded with the dust from the first two creature slayings, and now a dense fog filled the chamber. Nicholas saw the shadow of a figure clawing its way up and out of the wreckage.

The shadow figure in the cloud lifted its head. The dust was too thick, and Nicholas could not even tell if it was human. Nicholas waved his arms furiously to help clear the air and get a better picture of what he had set free.

"Nicholas?" a familiar voice asked from the shadow. "Is that you?"

Nicholas pushed his way through the debris and crouched down in front of the broken statue. He poked his head through the clearing dust and looked into the face of the mysterious shadow that had been trapped inside that awful sculpture. He knew this man.

"Dad?"

11

WHAT HAPPENED?

Thomas Bells grabbed Nicholas and gave him the biggest, longest hug ever. He might not have let go, but Nicholas needed to breathe, and he squirmed out of his father's mighty squeeze.

"You're not dead?"

"Apparently not. How long have I been gone, Nicholas?"

"A little over a year."

Dad's eyes watered. "I've missed you so much. Where's Sam? He was here with you that other time, wasn't he?"

"You could see us?"

Dad nodded. He was thinking about something else. "How's Mom?" he asked.

"Um . . . not so good, Dad. But you're back now, so everything will be okay again, right?"

Mr. Bells smiled. "Everything's going to be perfect. I promise."

"But Dad?"

"Yes, Nicholas?"

"What happened? How did you end up here?"

Dad stared into Nicholas's eyes, hoping that a simple look could recount an entire tragedy—but it couldn't. The story Dad told was worse than any nightmare.

On the terrible day of his disappearance, Mr. Bells woke up at six-thirty as usual. He showered, checked in on Nicholas and Tham, and left for work. Outside the apartment building, he heard the most peculiar screeching sounds from the side alley. Being a very curious dad, he went to investigate.

When he reached the alley, he discovered it wasn't a screeching at all. It was a conversation between two men with irritably high-pitched, scratchy voices. Imagine his surprise when he first laid eyes on Mr. Piddlesticks, hovering forty feet above the ground, conversing with his own stomach. Yes, the very same Mr. Piddlesticks we know and love.

111

Massive wings, attached to Mr. Piddlesticks's shoulder blades, held him in the air—not pretty, feathery bird wings. No, these looked more like thin membranes draped over an intricate skeleton. Totally gross. And he was standing—no, floating—right outside Nicholas and Tham's bedroom. Dad moved closer to hear what they were talking about.

"There they are," the beast told his belly. "No magic is more powerful. We must own them."

Dad was not about to let that beast enter his sons' room. Hoping that this was a reasonable creature, Dad figured maybe they could work something out. He was prepared to do anything to ensure that his boys were not harmed.

"Hey, you there," Dad yelled up to the . . . thing. Mr. Piddlesticks turned its faces and glared down at Dad.

"Come down here," Dad invited. "Let's talk face to face . . . to face." The wings fluttered and the beast drifted down to the ground.

"Yes?" it demanded imperiously.

"Whatever it is that you are looking at through that window, I'll give to you. We can handle this business, me and you, and no harm has to come to anyone."

Now imagine Dad's surprise when he learned that the monster wanted to pluck the freckles from his eldest son. He refused, of course, and bravely demanded that the beast leave. Mr. Piddlesticks, however, had other plans.

"If you won't give them to me then your son will be persuaded."

Dad laughed at that. "There's no way Nicholas will ever give away his freckles. I won't let him."

Mr. Piddlesticks snackled. "I hardly see what *you* have to do with it." Dad was about to reply to the creature, but he was suddenly whisked away to the dungeon and wrapped in stone. How? He still didn't know. He just knew that one second he was a dad, and the next he was a sculpture in some monster's basement.

"But you saved me, Nicholas. Now we can go home." Dad tapped his boy on the nose and asked, "So what are these funny, runny ink spots?"

"Oh no!" Nicholas looked at his watch. He had been so absorbed in his father's story that he had forgotten his mission. "It's twelve minutes after three!"

"So?"

"So, Mr. Piddlesticks will be back any second. I

still have a hundred and forty-nine dots to draw on myself before I can get my freckles back."

"Get your freckles back?"

"Shhh!" the two women warned. "Listen."

A *du-dump du-dump du-dump* sound was approaching. Nicholas looked to the winding staircase and saw the growing shadow of Mr. Piddlesticks.

"We have to hide," Nicholas whispered. "Now!"

He grabbed the six-hundred-year-old petrified earthworm, thumbed through the manual to find the spell he had to recite, and ripped the page right out of the book.

The *du-dump du-dump du-dump* was getting closer. Now it sounded more like *stimp-stomp stimp-stomp stimp-stomp*. Dad pushed Nicholas under the table, then found a hiding place for himself.

One more twisty turn of the stairs and Mr. Piddlesticks would discover the chaotic destruction of the three demolished statues. A blind man could not have missed the mess in that room. There was going to be trouble.

"What is this?" Mr. Piddlesticks's piercing voice trembled with rage. One of his oversized feet kicked a piece of marble across the room, launching it straight at Nicholas's head. He hugged the floor and the marble shattered to bits on the wall behind him. Afraid even to breathe, Nicholas got to work.

149.
148.
147.
146.
145.
144. . . .

12

THE DUEL

Mr. Piddlesticks plowed through the rocky mess that covered his floor. His anger bubbled out of every orifice in his body. When he burped, flames blasted out of his nostrils. He spoke out loud as he moved through the room.

"If you three come out now, I will not punish you. But if I have to come looking, you'll all wish that you never gave up the comfortable security of life inside your stone sarcophaguses. That I promise you."

Nicholas continued to draw freckles, apparently safe for the moment. Mr. Piddlesticks aimed his threat at three people. He did not realize that Nicholas was responsible for the destruction—let alone that he was in the room. Dad barely breathed so as not to disturb the bookshelf that he had wedged himself behind. He had no intention of turning himself in, and neither did the two women, one of whom squatted behind the cracked base of a statue while the other huddled underneath the very pile of rubble on which Mr. Piddlesticks now stood to address his prisoners again.

"You are trying my patience. I know that you are all in here. Hide as long as you like, there will still be no way out. This is your last chance. Show yourselves now and escape an eternity of discomfort and despair worse than anything you can imagine."

Mr. Piddlesticks knew he was a pretty intimidating guy, and he figured that if he laid the threats on nice and thick, his three escaped convicts would cave and turn themselves in, saving him the trouble of finding them. Then, he would most likely snackle and encase them all in new statues, where he would leave them for the rest of time.

But he was wrong. His dramatic threats were ignored. His prisoners knew that revealing themselves only guaranteed a swift return to their previous dismal fates. They would rather risk Piddlesticks's wrath for the chance to reclaim their old lives. There was, of course, no reason to believe that they would be able to escape, but free from the statues, they were closer than they had ever been.

"Fools!" Mr. Piddlesticks shrieked. "Have it your way!" He opened the sack around his neck and addressed the freckles inside. "Get out here! I need you." The freckles obeyed and filed out of the sack. They floated before their master and awaited instructions.

"Produce those three troublesome mates,
to cower before me and my hate!"

All 5,792 freckles came alive. They split into three teams and ventured forth. Team A bore through what was left of the base of the alligator-headed statue, converged on the trembling woman who was hiding there, lifted her up into midair, and flew her across the room. They dropped her in front of Mr. Piddlesticks and hovered above her, guarding their prize.

Team B squeezed through the cracks of a pile of rubble and swallowed the miserable woman who was lying there, only to fly her across the room and spit her out on top of her companion. Team B joined Team A and hovered above the captured prisoners.

Team C went around the bookshelf, making sure not to tarnish its finish or upset its balance—which pleased Mr. Piddlesticks—and seized Thomas Bells. They dragged him over the jagged edges of the debris that filled the room and left him slumped on top of the two women. They then led their brethren back into Mr. Piddlesticks's sack.

The prisoners stared up at Mr. Piddlesticks. He rubbed his hands together like a mad scientist. He glared down at them with his dark eyes. He flashed his yellow teeth. He cleared his throat and spit on them.

None of the prisoners noticed that beyond Mr. Piddlesticks's legs, on the floor across the room, Nicholas was tearing off his right sneaker and sock. He drew the final three replacement freckles on the bottom of his right foot—not left, not wrong, right. He was now ready to say the spell.

Mr. Piddlesticks screamed at his prisoners again. The sudden hollering caused Nicholas to jump back against the wall, knocking over a large rock. Mr. Piddlesticks shot a quick glance over his shoulder, but there was nothing to see. He refocused on his three fugitives.

"Tell me! How did you escape?" They did not answer. "Do you three insignificant weasels dare defy me?" Again no answer. "Speak now," Mr. Piddlesticks demanded, "or suffer for eternity."

While Dad and the women considered their options—suffer eternally or rat out Nicholas and then, most likely, suffer eternally—Nicholas faced a new problem. The spell was under the large rock. Nicholas attempted to move the giant rock, but it was too heavy. If Mr. Piddlesticks turned around, Nicholas was doomed for sure.

"Well?" Mr. Piddlesticks asked Dad and the ladies. They all sat there with nothing to say. "Fine, don't tell me. Don't say a single word, see if I care. But seeing how you're all of one mind on the subject, I think you should all be of one body, too.

> "*Magic freckles,*
>   *one,*
>   *two,*

three,
give these worms some unity!"

The freckles dutifully filed out of their pouch and circled around their victims. They moved faster and faster, forming an angry tornado—and poor Dad and the women were stuck in the center. The wind howled through the small dungeon.

At that very moment, Nicholas shoved a wedge of marble from the alligator-headed statue between the ground and the stubborn rock, boosting it up just enough to grab the spell. Mr. Piddlesticks, who was too busy enjoying the stormy weather, did not hear the noise.

The freckles were creating a hideous beast—an enormous earthworm with three heads—Dad's and the two women's. Dad tried to say something, but he and the ladies no longer had tongues. He looked over at one of the women in disbelief. You would be shocked, too, if someone suddenly turned you and two other people into a three-headed, tongueless worm.

Mr. Piddlesticks snackled at this wonderful sight: his beast, surrounded by his 5,792 freckles.

Across the room, Nicholas recited the spell:

"I now command you
Freckles, by Gewgaw's power—
listen, my servants."

Nicholas did not notice that the freckles turned to face him.

"All right, freckles," Piddlesticks said, "back in the sack." But the freckles did not respond to him. They hung in the air like stars. They were receiving higher orders—from the boy with the Gewgaw, who continued, undetected, to recite his spell:

"Forsaken freckles
given away,
the Gewgaw
will claim what is mine today.

Freckles, once mine,
seek inky dots,
and like Valentines
embrace those spots.

Freckles,
just speckles,

that's all you'd be
if not for the Gewgaw and its master—me."

The freckles, obedient servants that they were, congregated into one big cluster before Mr. Piddlesticks's eyes. Though annoyed by their delay, he was pleased to see that his freckles had finally come to their senses and decided to return to their sack. Imagine his rage when they flew right past him.

"Hey!" Mr. Piddlesticks screamed. "Get back here!"

He turned to see where his freckles were going—and saw Nicholas standing at the other end of the room. The Gewgaw glowed a fiery red in his witch eye. The 5,792 freckles swarmed Nicholas. They aligned themselves around him, and then, all at once, merged with their corresponding inky spots.

Nicholas examined his arms. His freckles, his precious freckles that he had taken for granted and hated his entire life, were back.

"Hold on," Mr. Piddlesticks screamed, "you can't do that. We have a contract." He pulled the parchment out of his blazer and held it up.

"So?" Nicholas confidently asked.

"So," Mr. Piddlesticks whined. "So there are rules and laws that cannot be broken."

"Okay," Nicholas conceded, "sue me." And with that a freckle launched from the tip of his nose like an explosive arrow. Bull's-eye! It struck its target and the contract ignited like a torch. The freckle returned to its master and settled onto his nose.

"Whoa!" Nicholas exclaimed. He had even surprised himself. "That rocked!"

"You can't break a valid contract!" Mr. Piddlesticks objected.

"True enough. But you obviously haven't read your manual," Nicholas explained. "At the very end of Chapter Ten, it says that the person with the Gewgaw can reclaim the freckles at any time. That's why the manual strongly recommends when cheating innocent children out of their magic, make sure to get the Gewgaw." Nicholas smiled.

"Get the manual, you moron," a muffled voice screamed at Mr. Piddlesticks.

"Shut up, you parasitic idiot!" Mr. Piddlesticks ripped open his shirt and screamed back at the face on his belly. Then Mr. Piddlesticks grabbed the manual and began to riffle through it in search of a defense.

"Sorry, Piddlesticks," Nicholas explained, "but I don't think I want you reading that right now." Two freckles, one from each of Nicholas's ears, took to the air. One barrel-rolled left and dropped underneath the book, launching the manual into the air. The other freckle intercepted the flying book and slammed it shut so hard that the magic volume collapsed in on itself and disappeared.

Nicholas watched Mr. Piddlesticks, who now looked like a wild animal who just woke up to find his mother had been shipped off to some zoo. The strange man with the backward knees and the face on his belly seemed rather pathetic standing there without his contract, his freckles, or his manual, overshadowed by his own monstrous creation.

If the story ended right now, Nicholas would have walked away from the dungeon, and that would be that. But Mr. Piddlesticks wasn't prepared to say "The End." In fact, he would have liked to bounce our friend Nicholas right through the wall of that slimy dungeon. So he launched himself across the room, ready to fight.

But Mr. Piddlesticks couldn't even get near Nicholas. The freckles had no intention of allowing that desperate man to lay one gruesome finger on Nicholas. They met Piddlesticks's attack with their own and engulfed the enemy, who disappeared in the freckled ocean with a stifled scream and a puff of smoke. And that was the last time Nicholas, or anyone else for that matter, saw Mr. Piddlesticks. Where the freckles sent him is truly a mystery.

However, I think it's safe to say that Mr. Piddlesticks is not alone in exile, for at the very moment that he vanished, so did the two Cosmetics Ladies, who were upstairs busily gossiping with their biggest customer. Mom, baffled and bewildered, rubbed her eyes and said to herself, "Darn flu."

The freckles triumphantly danced across the room, settling back into their favorite spots on Nicholas. Their unexpected adventure was finally over, and the freckles seemed happy to be in their rightful place, properly appreciated. It was a wonderful homecoming.

13

HAPPILY EVER AFTER

With a wink of his eye and a tap from his freckles, Nicholas unraveled Dad and the ladies. Their nightmare was really over. It was time for everyone to go home.

Mom, meanwhile, was up at the makeup counter, covering her freckles, trying to figure out what had become of the two Cosmetics Ladies. She blinked when her eyes played another trick on her—Nicholas seemed to emerge from the floor. Poor Mom was so terribly confused—all day people kept appearing and disappearing. It was extremely difficult to keep up with.

"Nicholas?" Mom asked, "is that really you this time?"

"It's me, Mom. Really."

Before his mom had a chance to ask questions, like what he was doing magically rising from the floor and where his brother was, she fainted. Was she *that* sick? Not really. She was probably overcome when she saw her supposedly dead husband rising from the floor behind Nicholas.

She came to at the sound of her husband's voice. "Lizzy. Lizzy. Come on, wake up."

She refused to open her eyes. "I don't talk to crazy, talking hallucinations," she said.

"Lizzy?"

There was no denying that that voice was real. She opened her eyes.

"Thomas? Thomas, is that really you?" Dad bent over and kissed Mom on the forehead. "It is you, isn't it?" And then Mom started to cry.

"What's wrong, Lizzy?" Thomas asked. "Why are you crying?"

"I don't know," Mom told him. "Because you're supposed to be dead." Dad took a good look at his wife, her face half-covered in goopy, gloppy freckle-covering creams. He started to laugh.

"Lizzy, what have you done to your freckles?"

"You hate me, don't you?" Mom cried through her tears. "I'm not Lizzy anymore."

"You're not?" Thomas asked, confused. "Then who are you?"

"I'm Elizabeth Dahling." Dad just laughed.

"Will you stop laughing!" Mom demanded. "What's so funny?"

"You," Dad answered. "You're so funny. I love your freckles, no matter what your name is, and"—Dad took a whiff of her obnoxious perfume—"no matter what you smell like."

"You do?"

"Of course."

"You mean you didn't leave because of my freckles?"

"No!"

"Mom," Nicholas jumped in, "my freckles can turn you back into your old freckle-loving self in less than a second."

"No!" Dad insisted. "It's nice of you to offer, Nick, but your mother and I don't need your magic. We have enough of our own."

(It may sound a little sappy, but what can I say—Nicholas's parents hadn't seen each other in a year, and that's the kind of cheesy stuff adults say to each other.)

Mom was feeling out of the loop. "Your freckles can do magic?"

"Don't worry," Dad assured her, "we'll explain everything to you later. Let's go home."

"Hold on," Nicholas said. "I have to go back to school."

"But school ended an hour ago."

"I know, but Tham's waiting for me. Besides, there's one more little mess that I have to clean up."

It was actually a huge mess. When Nicholas got back, the schoolyard looked like a circus. Parents who came to pick up their children were frozen in shock as they watched their mutant children running in circles, picking on each other. Theo Geisel, now a walking, talking tuba, belted out a deep bass and knocked Ali Lynch, a girl with twenty feet, onto her side. Vanessa, the vegetarian girl turned double cheeseburger, spit a wad of ketchup in Tony the Cyclops's only eye.

Other parents, more angry than shocked, stormed the principal's office to demand answers to obvious questions like:

"Where is my child's head?"

and

"How come my eight-year-old daughter has a beard and mustache?"

and

"Who attached that motor to my son's torso?"

Unfortunately, the principal, who was in a cocoon and well on his way to becoming a moth, was unable to provide answers.

"I'm going to bring this up with the PTA!" one angry mother declared.

"My husband happens to be close friends with the superintendent," another woman threatened.

"I told my wife we shouldn't trust these public schools," a devastated father screamed.

Who knows how long all this craziness would have continued if Nicholas had not shown up? With one quick shake, he sent every one of his 5,792 freckles to work. They swept through the entire school—dancing through the cafeteria, tumbling through the gymnasium, slithering under desks, peeking into the janitor's closet, searching lockers, and making sure they didn't miss a single nook or cranny or afflicted student. And when they were done, the students and faculty of Greenacres

Elementary were all safe from Mr. Piddlesticks's nasty curse.

Parents and children poured out of the school, none of them understanding what had happened there on that day, all of them relieved that it was finally over. Elliot Arsham, backed by a mob of students, approached Nicholas.

Now, you probably expect to hear that Elliot Arsham finally learned his lesson and was about to apologize to Nicholas for the years of torment. Not quite.

"Look, everybody," Elliot announced, "Frecklette washed off her girly makeup, and now he thinks he can be one of us. Well, guess what? You're still just a freak of nature, you, you, you Amazing Frecktacle."

"Yeah," Oscar Mercein added, "Freckle Face!"

"That's right," Anabelle Edwards chimed in, "Polka Dot!"

And, so what? Some kids will never learn. But fortunately for all of us, others will.

"You know what, Elliot?" Nicholas said in total confidence. "You're right. I am the Amazing Frecktacle. And if I were you, I'd stay out of my way."

EPILOGUE

WHAT ABOUT THAM?

Hold on. I got so excited there that I almost forgot to tell you about Tham.

Well, like the other cursed kids and teachers, Tham was cured when Nicholas's freckles swept through the school. And the wartless Tham finally found his way outside to his brother.

"Nicholathe?" Tham asked. "You punctually did it, didn't you?"

"Yeah, Tham," Nicholas said, "I actually did it. Let's go home. I have a surprise for you."

That night, for the first time in over a year, Nicholas, Tham, Thomas, and Lizzy Bells all sat down together for dinner.

"Tho, Dad, wath it thcary inthide Thtid-dlepickth thtatue?"

Poor Dad couldn't understand a word Tham said.

"I'm thorry it'th tho hard to underthtand me," Tham explained, "but I thtill have a nawful number of peech throblemth."

Tham flashed a shaky smile. Nicholas had a wonderful idea. A freckle flittered off his finger.

"Hey, Tham, what did you just say?" Nicholas asked.

"I said," Tham insisted, "that I'm sorry it's hard to understand me, but I still have an awful number of speech problems."

Everyone stared at Tham.

"My lisp," Tham shouted. "It's gone. Did you hear that? I actually said *lisp*. Hello, Nicholas, my name is Sam. Ha ha! I can say your name, *Nicholas*. I can say my own name. I can say *Sam*. I can even say *say*."

Nicholas watched his brother bounce around the room shouting "Sam" over and over again. The look in Nicholas's eyes said it all. Surely there was nothing more amazing in this world than being a frecktacle.

And there you have it. The Bells sat around the table for hours, eating and listening to Nicholas's tale. And when Nicholas was all through, I had my marvelous idea. Cured of all my speech impediments and armed with a new vocabulary, I would now tell the whole world the incredible story of Nicholas Bells, my older brother, the Amazing Frecktacle.

ABOUT THE AUTHOR

On his first day of kindergarten, Ross Venokur was asked to come up with a word that both rhymed with his name and described him. Ross, a freckled boy with huge red hair, thought his name was boring, so he took some creative liberties and proudly proclaimed, "I'm Rorse the Horse." His creativity has been flowing ever since. Rorse, a native New Yorker, grew up to be a screenwriter who lives in Los Angeles. He can't wait to move back to New York.